CRUELTY GAMES

CRUELTY GAMES

Wendy Robertson

CHIVERS LARGE PRINT
BATH

British Library Cataloguing in Publication Data available

This Large Print edition published by Chivers Press, Bath, 1997.

Published by arrangement with Severn House Limited.

U.K. Hardcover ISBN 0–7540–3064–4
U.K. Softcover   ISBN 0–7540–3065–2

Photoset, printed and bound in Great Britain by
Redwood Books, Trowbridge, Wiltshire

Ding dong my castle bell
Farewell to my mother
Bury me in the old church yard
Beside my elder brother.

My coffin shall be white
Six angels by my side
Two to sing and two to play
And two to carry me soul away.

(*For skipping*...)

Cry baby cry
Put your finger in your eye
Tell your mother what you've done
And she'll give you a sugar plum.

(For saying...)

Child killer has more than two meanings...

CONTENTS

A BRUSH WITH A STRANGER

1979

'All right, sweetheart? Any damage?' The busdriver twisted sideways in the cab to get a clearer view of the chaos caused by Rachel Waterman's mistimed jump from the bus. Her foot had missed the bottom step; she had crashed full-length, exercise books exploding vigorously from the constraints of various plastic carriers.

Rachel stood up, pulling down her sheepskin jacket, stroking the soft surface to clear it of particles of soil. She could feel blood oozing from her left knee and the throbbing of an embryonic bruise on her right.

She shook her head. 'I'm fine. Don't you worry yourself.'

The lights of the bus faded into the distance, leaving her in the dim dark of the winter evening. She searched the shadows of the narrow pathway, retrieving the brightly-coloured books lurking under the hedge and behind a pile of paving stones, which had been stacked beside the bus-stand for some eighteen months now.

She made her way along the familiar road

with its tall narrow houses. These were no longer dark and gloomy as they had been when she was young. Many were smartly painted now, stylishly curtained by new people; young couples who had been moving into the district in the last few years; a process called, she believed, gentrification.

She hobbled around the bend onto the narrow path which led to her house. A child was moving along on the opposite side of the path ahead of her. His fair hair bobbed towards her, alternately lit and lost in the gleam of the street lamps. A boy of eleven or twelve. Powerfully built.

For a second she clutched the carriers closer to her side. Then she dropped them away, walking freely. What was it these days that you had to be frightened of children?

'Hey, Missis!' A light voice called out to her.

'Yes? What is it?' Her over-clear teacher's articulation cut into the gloom. She peered across.

The boy's mouth was opening and closing. But there was no sound.

'Speak up! What is it?' She might as well be calling to the moon.

Then the boy was running towards her. She could hear the heavy thud of feet. He passed her at speed, raking the bulky carriers out of her hand. Once again, within the space of three minutes, she was shortening the distance between herself and the ground. Once again, she was scrambling round for the bags and the books.

Shaking from head to foot now, she scrambled to her feet, brushing twigs from her shoulders with a trembling hand. A savage dart of cold pierced the back of her neck, right through the protection of her heavy coil of hair. She hurried through her gate and into the safe haven of her house.

Once inside she went across to the window and stacked the books on their table. She leaned across the table, peering through the window towards the old hedge. The lawn, uncontained by any fence, was deserted. There was no one on the old path.

A kid! I've had enough of kids, she thought. I've had them, kids, all week. Up to here. I've had them large and small, silent and noisy, pleasing and petulant. God save me from kids.

Rachel smiled a little, recognising her joke with herself. She loved her job; she loved the cycle of fresh-faced children who came through her hands each year. She even loved toiling away on committees, trying to improve the every-day life of those in Oak Ridge Schools. The fact that this left her with no time for her own life might be seen as an advantage for a single middle-aged woman whose only relative was a sister in a city hundreds of miles away.

The telephone rang.

'Rachel?'

'Elena! How lovely to hear you! I was just thinking of you.' She changed the telephone from one hand to the other and winced.

'Rachel. What is it? Are you all right?' The voice sharpened.

'I'm fine. Just took a bit of a tumble off the bus.'

'Tripping up again are you? Well, anyway, I'm zipping up North on the eight o'clock from King's Cross this evening. A buckshee weekend. Something about redesigning the rotas. I didn't ask too closely.'

'It'll be good to see you.'

'Well it will be a bit of a quickie, lover. I'll get in after midnight and I'm going off in the morning up to Alnwick. A certain chap has promised me a bit of riding.'

'Oh, has he?' Rachel breathed out, relaxing now.

'And I must take him up.'

'And you must take him up.' Rachel smiled. 'I'll see you then.'

'Don't wait up, lover, will you?'

'Do I ever?'

An hour later Rachel was sitting with the ritual pile of books to one side of her; the ritual gin and tonic to the other; the ritual marking pen poised in one hand, when there was a long over-sustained ring on the doorbell.

A tall thin young man stood at the door. He was sun-tanned with hair cut very close to his skull. A baby squirmed in his arms and a toddler clung to his hand.

'Miss Waterman?'

'Yes?'

There was a pause. She moved from foot to foot. The man stood there, staring at her.

He had thought of her as taller. But she had the same heavy hair, threaded with grey now. The same big eyes, almost too round. The same figure, too bulky at the top. 'I can see it's you, now. I was wondering if you were all right ... how you were?'

'I'm fine. I'm well. But...'

He laughed. 'You don't recognise me. You used to be my teacher. But then you must have taught thousands of kids by now.'

There was an accent. Australian, perhaps. Midlands. She scanned the narrow face. No spare flesh. There seemed to be no child within. If she did not see the child she would not recognise him. He was unrecognisable. 'I'm sorry,' she began.

'I thought maybe you'd like to see my children. This is Charlie. And the baby here is Sophie.'

He pushed the small boy forward. The child was round-faced with a lick of hair falling in a sweep across his brow, smiling up at her, red-cheeked and confident. His eyes were a curious light blue rimmed with silver.

Looking into the face, she felt a spurt of recognition and relaxed. 'You may as well come in.' Resignation made her brusque. This

5

did happen now and then. A compliment really, to be remembered after so many years. It was terrifying, the mythic image people sometimes generated in their heads, of teachers they had known. Sometimes the myth was good. Sometimes it was bad. But it was always strong.

The young man settled comfortably on the couch and watched her vanish through the middle door.

She moved thoughtfully around the tiny kitchenette, making the tea, pouring it out and setting a glass of orange squash alongside the two mugs.

As she handed drinks to the man and the little boy, she looked more closely at the child. Something was picking away at her mind. She prided herself at not forgetting a face. And there were thousands of faces now. Still, there was nothing in the man that struck a bell; nothing in the face, nothing in the voice.

'I'm really sorry. This is awful, I still can't place you. Your voice. You don't sound...'

'That'll be the Australian. I was there five years; back two years now.'

'Your name? Your name would help.' She was good at names. Reading them off the register for a year, day after day. The names became fixed.

'My name's Alex Van Dorn. Now. You won't recognise it. That's who I became. It was after somebody I once met.' He paused, his

6

head dipped over his coffee. 'Once, when I was young, it was Ian Sobell.'

Her cup turned inwards in her lap, but she ignored the stinging liquid as it burned her inner thigh. His cool pale eyes looked across at her as he hugged the baby to him.

She stood up, her face blank. 'Oh dear. Look at this skirt. I must get changed.'

It was there, the black space inside her. The void with the black centre and the dark edge. She could not put her mind to the centre of that huge black space. She would not.

Her movements, as she put on a clean skirt, were sluggish and slow. She dumped the wet skirt in the washbasket and went to the window to lean her hot head against the cold glass. Her inward eye turned outward. She blinked. On the edge of her garden, where it joined the old path, stood the boy who had knocked her over. He was looking straight up at her face, into her eyes.

She opened the window and leaned out see him more clearly. His clothes were bulky and rough; his hair was thick and unkempt. She was reminded of travellers' children who, depending on the season, might turn up at school.

She opened the window and leaned out. 'Just what was it that you wanted, young man?'

The boy's mouth opened but it seemed that only certain words emerged, like a radio going in and out of tune. 'M ... Missis ... tha sh'd kna' ... not evil, bad ... they shouldn't a done that. Not ... that.'

'What? What? Shout up, dear!'

'I need ... I canna...'

The steel window-fitting was digging painfully into her waist as she leaned out. She looked down to move its position. When she looked up, the boy was gone. Only the deep shadow of the bush in the old hedge was left.

She returned downstairs to find the man humming away, playing finger-games with the little boy.

'It's Ian Sobell, then!' she said brightly. 'How are you, Ian?'

Then she fainted.

*　　　*　　　*

Rachel sat up in bed, staring into the deep blackness of funeral velvet. She opened her eyes wider, stretching the lids, to gulp in, to encompass any fragments of light that might be out there. There were no fragments, not a single chink of light. The black velvet began to move in on her, to lick around her. She opened her mouth to shout. At first there was no noise, then at last, 'Mo—ther!'

The darkness thinned down, then receded. The room filled with grey-green shade; the light from the street-lamp filtered through the flowered curtains. She breathed slowly in the way Daisy Montague had taught her, and the room threatened her no longer.

When she saw the figure in the corner, the still-sustained meditation-state kept her calm.

It was the boy from the path. He moved forward. 'You alright, Missis?' His hands were hanging down in front of him, loose and ungainly. The knuckles were over-large and purplish red.

'Yes. I'm all right.' She pulled her duvet closer. 'What is it you want?'

'Ah wanted to tell tha'. I bin watchin' tha'. The one. You's be the one. Ah'll tell tha...'

A strong accent. She was right. A travellers' child. 'What is your name?'

'Ah's called Wales. Pip Wales.'

'And what will you tell me?'

'The game. About the game. They made me play, and they...' The voice was fading although the mouth was moving.

She frowned and shook her head. 'Speak up!' she shouted across a broad abyss, across the space to the moon. She blinked her eyes; he was getting harder and harder to see. 'Stay! Don't go!' Tears were falling down her face, blinding her to his image altogether. 'Stay!'

*   *   *

It was sixteen years since those disastrous events and Rachel Waterman's life now, though routine and pedestrian, was calm. True, it had taken her three years, hospital, and the ministrations of three therapists to understand something of the nature of what had happened to her and others at that time.

Daisy Montague, the third therapist, had come up with the most satisfactory, and for that reason the most simplistic explanation. Enough anyway for Rachel to get back to something of a life.

Daisy had leaned back in her chair and tossed back her thick glossy hair. She took off her spectacles and rubbed her tired eyes. 'Look at it this way, Rachel, the path that leads to murder is a wide one. Most of us tread it. Don't we all say at some time: "I could have killed him?" Or her? And for one fraction of a second we mean it. But the path we travel on is a broad one, and we can choose to move aside, and away from the pain and the hurt, and the parallel desire to hurt back in order to show that we are here; we exist.

'But for some people, this wide path splits and splits, like branching nerves in a muscle or a heart. For those people the way gets narrower and narrower and it seems to some that there are no choices; they are pushed and pummelled on by the seen and the unseen travellers who share their journey.'

Daisy replaced her glasses, in that single action reinstituting the grave competence meant sometimes to reassure, sometimes to deceive. 'Perhaps at that point a savage act such as this is the only, the inevitable way for them to go.'

Rachel tucked away her hankie and frowned. This was like her mother's argument only somehow worse, endorsed by this intellectual authority, this gravitas. 'You mean it's preordained, inevitable?'

Daisy shrugged. 'Not in the religious way. More like when you set a hoop rolling down a steep hill; almost impossible to stop.'

The yellow cookery timer on her desk pinged, reverberating in the quiet air. Daisy smiled a full-toothed smile at Rachel, a smile turned on like a lamp, accompanied by direct eye-contact, which seduced all her clients into thinking that here was a very nice warm person. 'There, Rachel. Our time is up. See you next week?'

Rachel gathered up her bag, tried to put on her coat, dropped the bag and scrambled to retrieve it again. 'I don't think so, Daisy,' she said vaguely. 'I'll need to get in early. Such a lot on at school next week. I'll ring.'

Outside she looked at herself in the mirror at the head of the stairs, tucked one unkempt curl back into her beret, put her shoulders back and set out to face another week, as she had faced many weeks, with Daisy's help. But going down the steep shabby stairs with their curling posters about saving whales and driving with care, Rachel knew she would not return. She had the skeleton of an answer to the thing and she'd have to make do with that.

Poor Daisy, she thought, no wonder she got tired, having to smile like that all the time, and listen by the hour to people's terrors and nightmares. What a life!

PART ONE

THE MAIN EVENT

If I lie and you do wrong
May the devil slit my tongue.

(For saying...)

CHAPTER ONE

WISE CHILD

1963

Ian Sobell watched as Tadger Smith put his bullet-head, flat and low, against the blue-veined red brick of the school wall so that his view was taken up by Tadger's tree-trunk legs and the blue denim straining hard against his broad backside.

Behind Tadger, on the tarmac, a queue of boys had formed in loose order. The whole group was under the instruction of Flicka Smith who had directed his more docile brother Tadger to head the 'horse'. Ian giggled to himself at the sight. They might just be a queue of lads standing ready to give that sturdy backside a good kick. Ian felt tight inside with his own little joke. He had reason to dislike Tadger Smith's backside; fat and foul-smelling.

Peter Simmers, the first boy in the queue, raised his hand, the thumb pointing to the sky. He shouted to Tadger: 'Hum dum dum, finger or a thumb?'

Tadger's growling voice emerged from its encounter with the wall. 'Thumb!'

A raucous cheer cut the morning air,

followed by a chorus of jeers and whistles. Peter Simmers, twisting his face at losing the 'guess', went forward to put his hands on Tadger's waist, his head down between the big lad's solid thighs.

There was a pantomime that Ian had gone to a long time ago, with Sandra and some bloke that was hanging around that time. This stupid horse of cloth and canvas was gallumphing and snorting round the stage, men's legs and big black boots showing underneath. Now, here were Tadger and Peter doubling up as a bloody pantomime horse.

Ian smiled to himself again and wondered what happened to your willy when you were down there being the horse. Was it pushed right forward or did it hang in the next lad's face? Did it get hard? Tadger's probably did. Ian had seen it do that in the lav. Tadger had shown it to him and said had he ever seen bigger? He'd made him touch it and laughed when he flinched. Then he'd made Ian bend down and did his party fart in his face. The other lads laughed then, and called Tadger a dirty bugger.

He had got hold of Ian by the neck. 'What am I, young'n? What am I?'

'A dirty bugger.'

'Well just you remember that. And watch out.'

Now another boy was heading up the queue. He raised his hand. 'Hum dum dum, finger or thumb?'

Peter Simmers, head down, shouted 'Thumb!'

A cheer ripped through the playground. The boy grinned, making further gestures with his upheld finger. Then he loped up to the double horse at a flailing speed and leapfrogged with such forward propulsion that he ended up face to the wall, on Tadger's broad back.

Ian lurked to the side of the queue, watching cautiously through the side of his eyes. One by one, the boys held up their hands and shouted the question. A right answer from the horse meant the caller had to come to be part of the snaky horse shape. If the horse guessed wrong, the caller had won and he could take a flying leap and join the riders. The force of some of the leapfrogs made the horse buckle, as the leaper smashed into the bodies in front of him.

Finally Flicka Smith, the last player, 'beat' the horse with a correct call. The horse waited for its final victor, swaying a little, held together by the powerful thighs of the earlier victors, the boys on top. Ian took the chance he'd been waiting for. Racing past Flicka, he did his own flying leapfrog onto the horse, that heaving mass of ten bodies.

Behind him a roar of rage went up. Beneath him the horse collapsed.

Flicka Smith raced across and hauled Ian

out of the struggling, worm-like heap. 'What the fuckin' 'ell d'ya think you're doing, kid?'

The bigger lads were standing up now, brushing themselves down, eyeing the intruder. Tadger came to stand beside Flicka.

Ian looked from one hulking brother to the other. The yawning gap between their size and his, their age and his, filled the air between them with a threat so solid you could have carved it into shape.

'What the fuckin' 'ell d'you think you're doin'?' Flicka repeated.

'Just havin' a go, Flicka.'

'Who asked yer?'

'Nobody.'

'Nobody? No-fuckin' body?' Tadger started to push Ian's shoulder, so hard that he stumbled backwards. One of the other lads caught him and he was pushed round the circle till he was dizzy and bruised. After a few minutes the pace slackened. He took the chance to get his head down and butt his way through the ring of bodies and bellyaches, and run.

*　　　*　　　*

The boys yelled wordless howls and grunts as they lolloped after him. Ian ran down an alley at the side of the school, zip-zapping past the bins and the two heaps of coke. A shot of pain like fire jabbed through his foot and up

18

through his leg. He hopped around, groaning.

The troop of boys encircled him.

'What's up?' grinned Tadger. 'Can't take it? Have to have a cry, have a bubble?'

'Here he is again,' sniggered Peter Simmers, 'In the daft class en't yer? Your teacher's the one with the big tits. Teaches yer to bubble doesn't she? She does. Soft as shit, the lot of yer.'

Ian wiped his palm across his face, smudging the tears away. 'Nah. Don't talk bloody soft. Stood on sommat. A nail.'

Flicka leaned up against the wall, his arms folded up behind him. 'Well that'll teach yer to join in where you're not wanted, kid. You go play with the other babbies, see?'

Ian said nothing.

Tadger looked down at him, and the others waited for their cue. Then the bell rang; he shrugged his massive shoulders and turned to go, the rest melting away after him.

Ian took a breath, then hobbled into school, using only the tip of his toe on the foot with the nail in it. The pain shot up into his head like a hot spike and he could feel the sweat pour down his back. He wiped his face with the back of his hand. Still though, it wasn't bad, was it? Taking Flicka's place on the long horse. Making the stupid thing collapse. Not half bad.

*   *   *

Rachel Waterman lifted her eyes from the road to the red-brick building at the top of the hill. Siskin School loomed like a faded castle from the dusty grey of the school yard, surrounded by a curtain wall embellished with white-painted goal-posts and multi-coloured bulls-eyes. It was, she knew, a dinosaur of a school: a survivor from an earlier age when five-year-olds still came to the same school building as their brothers and sisters. Radical notions such as secondary-modern, or the more recent comprehensive schools, had quite passed it by. There were rumours, always rumours that they were going to build a brand new school for Siskin. There were also other rumours: that they were going to demolish the whole blighted district of Siskin, so there would be no need for a school at all.

Still, for now, there were children to teach. She sighed hard as she steered carefully through the tall gates and parked her vehicle beside the others, which were clustered up against the wall like so many suckling piglets. There, under observation from the staff room, they were considered safe.

Rachel thought about her class. 2X: seventeen of them, bursting with energy and perpetually difficult to control. She had been landed with this class as the newest teacher on the staff with no power to choose. It had been fashionable for a while to teach them with the others. But even in this hard school, one after

20

another the teachers complained of disruption and anarchy. Apparently one even went sick. So Warner had gone back to the good old ways and withdrawn them for "special teaching". Miss Priestley, who had taught most of them the previous term, told her (not concealing a victorious smile), that half of them were bad, the other half mad, and there was nothing you could do with them.

'Withdrawal class? They need withdrawing from the school, if you ask me. Withdrawing from the human race.' Miss Priestley had expelled one of her neighing laughs. 'Anyway, they'll give you something to cut your teeth on, Miss Waterman. You'll learn or burn with that lot.'

Rachel was a quiet girl. She had never been the captain of the netball team at school, nor a leading member of the debating society. Her acceptance at her humble teaching college had been a surprise to her. She was not the type, anyone could see. They must have been hard-up for students. Nevertheless she had arrived at Siskin School at the beginning of this term, qualified, moderately keen, and appropriately scared. And to her surprise she was quite enjoying it.

Early in her acquaintance with this class, Rachel had realised that, as a whole body of people, she could not control them. They would do neither as they were asked nor as they were told. Rachel might not have been a born teacher but she was intelligent. So for her own survival, she began to build liaisons, one by one, with the children. She talked to them as individuals—in the playground, in the yard, in the corridors. She asked about their families, about music, what they did at night, their clothes, their possessions. Then, when begged to be quiet in the classroom, they were more likely to lapse into silence as a personal favour to her. Sometimes it worked, sometimes it didn't. It was all very exhausting. The times when the strategy didn't work were frequent.

Once, after a chaotic failure in the imposition of silence, she was given some kindly advice by Jane Brown, a buxom thirteen-year-old with a round white face and flat black pop-alley eyes. Jane always sat at the front, on the right.

'Why doncha do what Miss Priestley did, with the ones who talk too much, Miss?'

'What was that, Jane?'

'Sellotape. She stuck their mouths up with Sellotape.'

Rachel looked at Jane's closed, prim face. 'I don't think so, Jane.'

'I'm tellin' yer, Miss.'

At the very beginning, the headteacher, Keith Warner, had described 2X as 'a challenge':

'... and you are fortunate to have such a small class, Miss Waterman. You will keep them with you all day. More like a primary class. Build up their confidence. Build up their skills. The two go hand in hand.'

Mr Warner was tall and very clean about his narrow person: his face shone with cleanliness; his hands were always spotless, his nails white, sometimes bloody with scrubbing. His shirts were always snowy white; his tweed jackets had neat leather patches.

It had taken some time for Rachel to get used to the headteacher's strange customs. One instance was his habit of entering, unasked, into her classroom. On these visits he would stalk up and down the rows of high wooden desks. Then he would call across to her, in his high crisp voice, across the greasy tousled heads, the hunched shoulders: 'Who's smelling, Miss Waterman, who's smelling?'

She would shake her head innocently and he would put up his chin and let his nose lead him to some child, whose ear would be clutched between finger and thumb, the little finger daintily cocked. The child would be led off to be cleaned, reprimanded and lectured on the proximity of godliness and cleanliness.

Rachel could never understand how Keith Warner located these deviants. In her experience all the children shared the same rank smell. After two minutes in the classroom, her own sense of that smell was conveniently diminished. For her, during the classroom hours, none of them smelled. So, in these hours, like some kind of animal, she became

23

one of them; she took on the smell.

In the evening, when she finally got home from school, she was brought back into her outer world by the wrinkled noses of her mother and sister Elena. From her first day at school they had refused to sit with her until she had showered, changed her clothes and hung her school clothes on the line outside. She did not protest, but felt resentment, not just on her own behalf but on behalf of the children, whose pariah status was none of their fault, any more than it was hers that she had landed in that school with them. She was used to being a bit of a butt at home. The quiet sister, rather too large up top for the fashion now, and too buried in her books to attract the kind of male attention which would have pleased her mother in her voracious hunt for the father of her grandchildren.

*   *   *

'Miss Waterman, can you come and see Ian Sobell? Something wrong with his foot. And he's been crying fit to kill.' The harsh voice of Mrs Simmers, mother to Peter, penetrated the peeling door of the medical room. Ian winced at her tone of grim pleasure. Her work as dinner supervisor offered low wages and few pleasures, but bawling out children of whom she disapproved had a certain satisfaction.

The door opened, and Mrs Simmers, her

navy uniform crackling, bustled in, followed by Miss Waterman, tall and bony. Yes, he thought. Waterman does have big tits. Tadger's not wrong. And now her face had turned that fiery red which happened when things went wrong in the classroom. But she had dead smooth skin. Mebbe she was a teacher but she was not all that old. Maybe even younger than Sandra.

The medical room was a narrow cupboard beside the headmaster's study. It was furnished with a small chair, a low couch and shelf on which lay the locked medical box. The red cross on this old tin had faded now to pink and where before the tin had been white, it was now a scummy grey, burnished to a brown where the rust bloomed through.

Ian was sitting up very straight on the couch in his tee-shirt and battered jeans. His face was hard and cold. He bit his lip hard to quell the pain in his foot.

'What's up, Ian?' said Rachel.

'He stood on a nail in the yard, didn't you, Ian?'

He nodded, looking hard at his feet.

'But he won't take his shoe off, will you Ian?'

He shook his head.

Rachel knelt down beside him, pulling the bottom of his jeans away to one side. He wasn't wearing socks, so as he stared down he could see, just as she saw, the particular way that the dirt set into his ankles. She drew a breath, and looked up at him from her place on the floor. His face was dirty, his blond hair lank; his pale blue eyes had an odd ring of silver round the iris as they shone into hers.

'We'll have to have that shoe off, Ian. It would be a rusty nail. You could get infected.'

She lifted his foot. A small foot; Ian was small, even slight for his age. He looked younger than his twelve years. She could see the head of the nail on the ribbed sole of his shoe. She shuddered, feeling that nail going through the rubber into the soft flesh of his foot. She willed him, hard, to do as he was asked.

He shrugged, his lips still pinched together, then thrust his foot into her lap. 'All right, Miss.'

Nervously, she eased off the shoe. He breathed out, his mouth relaxing a little. Mrs Simmers clicked her mouth with disapproval.

His foot was black with dirt, which was set in very deep round the ankle and near the toes. The customary smell was much stronger. She turned his foot over. Blood was oozing from the puncture onto his blackened sole. Tears slopped around the edges of his wide eyes, but did not fall onto his face.

*   *   *

'Looks messy, Ian. You'll have to go to the doctor's for an anti-tetanus injection.'

26

'Anti what? What's that mean?'

'It'll stop your foot swelling up, and it'll stop your jaw locking.'

'Will it really? Does your jaw really lock?' His eyes cleared. The tense pain was leaving his face.

'I think so.' She wasn't sure whether people's jaws really did lock. 'Right! We need clean feet for the doctor.' She looked up at Mrs Simmers who was standing there with her arms folded. 'Any chance of a bucket of soapy water, Mrs Simmers?'

Rachel smiled deliberately up at the disapproving face. The smile usually worked. Mrs Simmers went off, stamping her anger into the worn tile floor.

An hour later, Ian was sitting beside Miss Waterman in her battered mini-van, directing her through the streets that mazed up up behind the school. He was feeling more cheerful now with a clean bandage on his foot and the shock of being pricked by the doctor's needle fading.

'Here, Miss.'

They turned a corner and stopped beside a door which had once been painted pale blue, and was now peeling and cracking. Initials were scratched in a fairly random fashion into the wood, showing the silvery scar of grain here and there.

Ian turned and looked up at her. 'Alright, Miss, now. I'll go in meself.'

'I'll have to see your mother, Ian. I have a form to fill in.'

He heaved a sigh. 'It won't be me mother, Miss. It'll be me Nana.' He pulled a key from his trouser pocket, and opened the door. 'Nan, it's me. The teacher's here.'

A tall woman still in her early forties, stood up from the fireside chair in which she had been sitting. She stubbed out her cigarette and smoothed back her hair, which had flopped down on one side.

'I hurt me foot,' said Ian. 'I been to the doctor's.'

She looked from him to his teacher then pushed past them both to go out into the hall.

'Sandra!' she called up the stairs.

Ian watched his Nana cautiously, wondering when the explosion would happen.

* * *

The clip of high heels was muffled only slightly on the thinly carpeted stairs. Rachel watched with interest as a young woman came through the door. Her hair was like spun glass, her skin white as milk and her eyes, like Ian's, pale blue with silvery rims. A cheap cotton wrap covered her slender figure. Even with her face creased with recent sleep, she had a rare beauty.

Ian stood up straighter as she came across to put her hand on his shoulder. 'This is my mam. This is Miss Waterman, my teacher, Sandra.'

28

There was a pause as Rachel processed her surprise. To be Ian's mother, this girl had to be around twenty-seven or eight, but she looked years younger than that. Even younger than Rachel herself.

The girl lit a cigarette, watching Rachel carefully, aware of her own impact.

'Sandra works at night, Miss,' said Ian.

'What's wrong? What's he done? He's not responsible, don't you know? He can be a little bugger, I'm tellin' yer. Not right … He's a bit…'

'He hasn't done anything wrong, Mrs … Miss … He's injured his foot in the playground and I needed to talk to you. It needs to be kept clean, really clean, or it will become infected.'

'Why, thank you,' Sandra said coldly, pulling Ian closer to her. Small as she was, he only reached her shoulder. He could smell her dusty perfumed smell; he could feel her soft shape against his side. 'Thank you anyway, for bringing him home.'

They stood there. Rachel moved from foot to foot. 'Well, I'll go.'

There were nods but no smiles. Ian looked at the floor.

She backed to the door and found her way outside and into the haven of her van.

*　　　*　　　*

'Miss Waterman? At last.' The narrow

wolfshead of Mr Warner loomed up as she raced back into school. 'That took longer than I would have thought. Now, I would be grateful if you would return to your class. I've given them some handwriting practice. I have to say their books are a disgrace.'

She scowled at him and said nothing.

'I can see no reason for gratuitous incivility, Miss Waterman. I will remind you that you are on your probationary year. And everything . . . everything . . . is noted.' He turned on his heel and stalked along the bare corridor to his room.

She followed him to the door and with meticulous care she placed an imaginary arrow into an imaginary bow and let it loose down the corridor towards his receding back. Then she went into the classroom which was unusually quiet. She beamed round. 'Now then 2X!' she said. 'What next?'

CHAPTER TWO

AT THE CROSSROADS

Ian leaned back and half-closed his eyes. He liked the big space of the hall with its echoing windows and its smell of sweat and dust. He liked the way Miss Waterman belted out the tunes, sea-songs alternating with swinging

30

Beatles songs. From his usual back bench he watched her long fingers bash away at the yellowing keys. He wriggled his bottom to the music, slithering to and fro on the polished wood. These were the same benches they used for balancing in PE. He liked that balancing thing, being up aheight. He was good at that. Really good. Being up aheight and looking down on the others. Nice, that.

His eye wandered across to the glass partitions that enclosed the hall like a cage, and caught the figure of Mr Warner as he stalked about the classrooms. The old boy would prowl his way into here soon. Always crossing the hall in a music lesson, he was. Nosey old bugger, fingering away at things.

The nice thing about Waterman was that she liked you to have a good shout. You could enjoy it. And she liked it even more if you added a few actions here and there.

Now she was picking out the opening bars of 'Little White Bull', a subversive choice in this school. The children in the back row shuffled about, linking arms, grasping shoulders and starting to sway. Ian, on the end, had his shoulder clamped by the broad arm of James Denton as they roared the chorus, bobbing away.

Rachel, glancing up at the glass partition behind the piano, saw Mr Warner set off from the far corner of the hall, his thin lips folded tight. As he drew level with Ian, a strong shove

31

rippled along the row, into the large frame of James Denton, who toppled against Ian, crashing him to the floor at Warner's feet.

Blinking to shut out the image, Rachel put her eyes back on the music and played on. But she couldn't resist turning round. The headteacher's shining white face flushed pink as he dipped his long body to pull Ian Sobell up from the floor by the back of his tee-shirt. He hauled him, kicking and struggling, to the back of the hall. Rachel thumped and thumped away at the piano, children's voices trailing behind her in a muted rendering of 'Little White Bull'.

From the piano Rachel could see the back of the hall, where Mr Warner was shaking Ian, saying something to him in a low, intense voice. Ian responded. Mr Warner raised his white hand with its clean nails high and swung a blow at Ian, who ducked. The blow entirely missed him, but was delivered with such violence that the headmaster overbalanced and fell to his knees.

The image fixed itself to the edge of Rachel's vision: Ian Sobell gazing numbly down at Mr Warner on all fours, and continuing to watch as he slowly and painfully staggered to his feet, and then limped towards the sanctuary of his room.

She played on, bashing the notes with some vigour, biting her lips to keep her deep forbidden laughter safely down inside her.

Mr Warner's accident caused him to be away from school for the first time in his forty-year career. In those weeks it seemed that the school was having an internal holiday. There was more noise about the place, even though the atmosphere was calmer.

Jack Marriott, Warner's deputy, was now in charge, striding about the place like a roaring, if rather toothless tiger.

Observing Miss Waterman, Ian noted that she laughed more and she stopped nagging, stopped begging and begging, please, for silence. There were no more and no fewer riots in the classroom, but there was less tension.

One morning, two weeks after the unfortunate accident, class 2X were faced with a beaming teacher. She looked so pleased that they all quietened down out of sheer curiosity.

'On Wednesday, we're going out for a walk,' she said excitedly.

They groaned as a matter of principle.

She beamed on, her thickish lips pulling back from her large teeth. 'Now, no groaning.'

Ian thought about how white her large teeth were and how much he liked the bright green dress she was wearing: the collar was embroidered with red flowers and it had long sleeves which pulled against her sharp elbows.

'What we're going to do, 2X, is walk the area within the square half-mile of the school, on a voyage of discovery.'

There were only one or two moans this time. To be out of school, for any reason at all, couldn't be all bad.

She smiled round at them again, relieved. 'We'll make notes and records of anything we find which is of interest. Then we'll make a—a—wall chart, or something, to show off our work.'

*   *   *

On Wednesday, in spite of her warnings about wearing strong footwear, the children came in their usual assortment of gear: ragged sandshoes and boots for the boys; the usual flimsy shoes for the girls. Jane Brown came in high-heeled sandals and wore blue eye-shadow. Rachel looked her hard in the eyes, but refrained from comment.

As they finally set out, Rachel gave a thought to Mr Warner, imprisoned on a bed in his sitting room. He would have lectured her about the need—'... Miss Waterman, to contain, to control, to police...'

Well, here they were, tramping towards the old swimming baths in good order, notebooks in hand. They walked in a decorous crocodile, two by two. She looked uneasily along the prim virtuous faces, not believing her luck.

Ian Sobell walked at the head of the crocodile, beside Rachel. He was walking very gingerly. 'Is your foot hurting, Ian?'

'Not much, Miss.'

'Did you hurt it?'

'It was from that nail, Miss. The one that got through my trainer.'

'But that was ages ago, Ian! Is it swollen?'

'Just a bit, Miss.'

'Didn't you go back to the doctor's then, like he said?'

'No. I couldn't. Me Nana had a bad back, that day, see?'

'Time you started doing things for yourself, my lad. Will you let me have a look at that foot, when we get back to school?'

'If you want to, Miss.'

They stopped at a broad iron gateway set in a high stone wall. 'This is the entrance to the old baths. See? Over the gateway?' she said.

They gathered round. There was a scuffle at the back as one boy climbed on another to get a better view.

'Who can tell me what it says?'

Jane Brown put her hand up then spelled out the elaborately carved stone letters: PUBLIC BATHS.

Leaning his face on the pock-marked rusty iron, Ian could see through the gates to the inside. He was disappointed. Only a few old heaps of stone, some straggling grass and a high wall.

Rachel shushed them so they would hear her. 'It seems they were built in the 1920s.

People from round here collected the money for the building themselves. Everybody helped—with the construction as well: done by people who were unemployed at the time.'

'Looks like a right dump now, Miss,' offered Mamie Johnson cheerfully. 'Mebbe the doleys down the town could build it up again.'

Assisted by Ian and James Denton, Rachel made a gap by pushing hard at the chained gate and they all squeezed through. Once inside, they trickled across the open space, overgrown with weeds and wild shrubs which had taken rampant possession of the cracks in the old stone. They had flourished through the years under protection of the high stone walls.

'It's like a bloody jungle, Miss,' said Ian.

'Isn't it just?' she agreed absently.

She gave them all specific tasks: drawing different plants; sections of wall; views out towards the town.

Mamie and Jane raced around clicking away with Rachel's newfangled Polaroid camera. She showed James Denton and some others how to create rubbings from the crumbly walls and the bark of the mean trees which sprouted from the stone floors.

James looked, in some puzzlement, from the paper in one hand to the soft pencil in the other. Large for his age and clumsy-handed, James had spent a good deal of his life in some state of puzzlement. He was hard to teach; he could barely read or write and could only concentrate for thirty seconds at a time. His mother had strenuously and successfully resisted efforts to have him taken to another, even more special school.

From the beginning Rachel thought James was quite nice to have around. He smiled a lot. He filled a comfortable amount of space. He liked everyone, and would carry things from place to place with some efficiency. Apart from that he benefited very little from school.

Rachel took James away by himself, to a section of stone wall in a corner and showed him again how to tackle the job of taking rubbings from surfaces. There was a glimmer of light in his eyes and he gave her a sweet smile. 'Like that, Miss? I can do that.'

So he could. He used dozens of sheets of soft paper, taking rubbings from all kinds of surface on the building, the tip of his tongue well out of the corner of his mouth.

Ian walked over to watch him, picking up the finished papers, tipping them this way and that to catch the light.

James smiled down at him. 'Look at this Ian. I can do it.'

'I can see that, Jimmy . . .'

'Ian Sobell, will you get on with your job and leave James to his?'

'OK, Miss. Hold your horses.'

Rachel broke open and distributed a pack of plastic bags to hold the samples they were collecting: a piece of stone or wood, a plant, anything of interest. She could hear the haunting echo of Mr Warner's voice, chanting its litany about never trusting them, about their natural predisposition to vandalism and stealing.

By eleven o'clock, they were finished. 'School! We have to get back to school! We've got to get back to school.' Her call for them to stop was greeted with the expected chorus of moans.

'Can't we go back the long way?' begged Jane Brown, her black eyes snapping up at Rachel.

'Yeah, Miss,' said Ian. 'If we go up round the top of this road, we can turn back up there at the cross-roads, where the bus stops. I've never been up there. Then down the hill, then up Creadon Hill and back to school.'

'Come on, Miss.'

'Yes, Miss, yes!'

'Yes, Miss, yes!'

The bubble of sound floated from one mouth to the other and grew and grew. The faces, many too fat or too gaunt for real health, looked up into hers.

She shrugged and nodded. The tumult died down. 'But only if you keep in your twos and walk properly.'

'But only if you get into twos and walk nicely!' mimicked Jane. But still she moved to pull her friend Mamie into line beside her.

There was a good deal of puffing and

blowing by the time they arrived at the crossroads and clustered together on the pavement by the traffic lights. They blocked the path of a woman walking her dog. The woman glared, edged around the crowd and stalked away, muttering away to her pet.

Rachel stood looking around her. 'Now, has anyone been up at the crossroads before?'

'I passed on the bus once, Miss,' volunteered Ian. Other heads were shaken in silence.

'See how both roads cross here, how they lead down from here? You can see the town, can't you? What can you see?'

'There's the Town Hall, Miss.'

'There's the Dole.'

'There's our school...'

'And what do you see behind?' Rachel questioned.

Long Ridge, from which Oak Ridge got its name, swept away behind the town, rolling and dipping like folded cloth.

'It's like, hills, Miss.'

'What are they called?'

The collection of blank faces stared up at her again.

'Have you really never been up there?'

Another slow shake of heads. These children lived in a territory of three or four streets, bound in by poverty or sheer lack of will to move further afield.

Ian looked up at her. 'Can we take the short-cut back down, Miss? See that path by the hedge?'

They looked down past the hedge towards the narrow pathway. It was overgrown with grass, but marked in shadow like a faint pencil line. She remembered Ian's injured foot, and his limping gait. 'All right. I suppose that way will be shorter, perhaps more interesting. But we'll have to do it in a particular way,'

The pale faces looked up at her, waiting for words in a rustling silence. Warner would like this, she thought. Absolute order, absolute control. 'Will you do it in this particular way?'

Nods all round.

'We must go single file, like the great forest hunters did in North America. One by one and totally silent. And we must listen, to see what we can hear. Then save it in your heads till we get back to school and you can tell us all about it. What do you hear? Use your ears...'

They followed her instructions to the letter. Ian led at the front; she followed at the end of the line. They made their way along the narrow path in complete silence. She could hear the birds; the busy rustling of the hedge creatures.

The Indian file suddenly congealed into a lump of bodies as they came to a small clearing, entirely stripped of grass. Here the only growing thing was a large thick-trunked elm, its branches jutting at awkward angles, totally bare of leaves. The ground around it was hard bald clay. They were all standing around in silence when Rachel finally arrived bringing up the rear. Only James Denton was still bustling about, pulling out paper and stubby pencil to taking a rubbing from a stone which was on the edge of the clearing.

'What are you stopping for?' Rachel whispered, carrying their silence into herself.

'Can you hear it?' said Ian. 'Can you hear?'

She listened to the silence. She could hear nothing. 'Nothing,' she whispered. The rising tide of temper and impatience died in her when she realised the truth of what she had just said. She could hear nothing; not a bird, although it was May; not the rustle of a leaf, although around them the hedges were in full bloom.

Ian's ears twitched at the people around him as they breathed louder and stronger. Tom Carling, always nervous, started to cry. A thick fog of panic rose amongst them and seemed to whirl about. Ian felt he could taste it, like soap on his tongue. Then the hair at the back of his neck prickled and he started to sweat.

'Now!' Miss Waterman's loud voice, belled into the silence. 'This is very interesting isn't it? A bare space and this big tree. It's an elm. You know, these big trees have been dying all over England in the past year or so. Such a pity. Such lovely old trees. But there's nothing growing on the ground, either'. She paused. 'And no sound.'

'There's sommat queer about this place, Miss,' said Mamie.

'It *is* odd. We'll check it out when we get

41

back. Look in the books. We'll check about the elms, and we'll check about this place. Come on, come on. Let's get on. At this rate our dinners will be cold.' Rachel was very brisk and her voice sounded very loud, almost bellowing.

Energised and relieved, they began to move on.

This time Rachel took the head of the line, walking alongside Ian on the widening path.

He looked up at her. 'Didn't you hear it, Miss?'

'You mean the silence? Yes. It was strange, wasn't it?'

'No. That cry. Like, a big cry. Mebbe a cat. I heard cats mek that noise. Or mebbe some lad's voice cryin' out. I heard that before too. You hear it?'

'No, Ian. I didn't hear any voice. To me it was just very very quiet.'

'There *was* a voice, Miss. A lad's voice crying out. Didn't you hear it?'

CHAPTER THREE

SPOONFEEDING

When 2X arrived back at school, the central hall was jammed with long tables; the top table crammed with great aluminium tanks of food prepared at the central kitchen that morning.

The place smelled of boiled potatoes and stale cabbage. Children were crowded onto the benches. Knives and forks rattled and drummed on bare tables.

With the children packed together, the strong body smell was distilled to a greater intensity. This was intermingled with a food smell which, on her first day on dinner duty, when she was still noticing smells, had reminded Rachel Waterman of the potato peelings her Uncle Henry boiled each week for his pigs.

Most children at Siskin had free dinners, although Mr Warner himself and most of the teachers never actually consumed school food. The headteacher gained his lunchtime sustenance by prowling round the edge of the hall, clipping an ear here, a head there, occasionally blowing his whistle for a minute's complete silence.

When Rachel Waterman first witnessed this drama, her undisguised smile was treated by a furious glare from Warner.

On the day that 2X went on their walk, Jack Marriot was on duty, barking away. Having seen her children safely onto their glaringly empty table, Rachel slipped into Mr Warner's study to rake over his sparse, highly-polished shelves. She could find only two books about Oak Ridge. One, twelve years old, in a series called Local Studies, was simply entitled 'Oak Ridge'. The other was called 'A History of Oak

43

Ridge', and had been published in 1890.

Back in the staff room, she munched her crisps as she tucked paper markers in all the places where the crossroads were mentioned.

Miss Priestley peered at her over her glasses. 'Spoonfeeding again, Miss Waterman?'

Rachel turned her shoulder to get the peering face out of her line of vision and went on reading. She munched on. It seemed that the crossroads were historically significant as a high point in the area. They were located at an important crossing place where the major road from Durham to the West was crossed by a minor North-South road. Gipsies still gathered there regularly on their way South for the Appleby Fair. They would only, however, make camp on the North side. They avoided the South side; something about an old place of hanging.

With her usual care, Rachel went on slipping in the paper markers. She was impervious now to the accusation of spoonfeeding. This meticulous preparation was another way she had found to make her own day-to-day life easier.

In the afternoon, 2X set about recording everything they had discovered that morning. Bits of stone and wood were pulled out of plastic bags; sketches and scribbled descriptions were referred to; words noted were linked into quite rough and simple sentences. Samples of leaves and plants were looked up in dog-eared reference books that had lived for some years on the corner shelves in the classroom.

Rachel put James Denton in charge—a new experience for him—of Tom Carling and Mamie Johnson. They were to mount the stone texture rubbings on black paper. James set to with a will, flourishing the paper with his clumsy hands and giving soft orders to the other two.

Rachel called out above the growing tumult. 'And I have two books here, for reference. About the geography and history of places we've been this morning. We need to go through these to see if we can find anything useful. Any offers?'

Ian looked at the way the long sleeve of her dress fell away from her bony hand. He put his hand up. The other raised hand was that of Mary Charters, the best reader in the class.

Mary took the environment book. Ian took the history book, a green volume bleached out to fawn at the edges, frayed at the corners. He turned it round in his hands, rubbing across the worn leather with greasy palms.

'Are you sure you'll manage this, Ian?'

'Course I can...'

'Yes, I suppose you can. You're a funny one Ian. Never pick up a book from one month to the next. But you can do it if you want to. If only—'

But he had opened it at the first place that

45

Rachel had marked and his head was tucked down over the page.

Every head was bent down over some task of drawing, writing, reading or mounting. Rachel looked around and smiled faintly.

After ten minutes Ian came out to her at her desk. 'I found a bit to copy here, Miss.'

'Have you, Ian?' She tried not to show how pleased she was in case it put him off. It was so rare for him to volunteer anything. 'Have you got some paper?'

'Miss, there's no way I can do this!' Wendy Burroughs was shouting to her across the classroom, tears in her eyes. Rachel pushed some clean sheets hurriedly towards Ian, then went across suggest to Wendy that she use the Polaroid photographs to help her with the problem of drawing the Old Baths.

After that she went and sat beside James and his stone rubbings. Cut out irregularly and mounted on black they were looking quite fine. James was proud of them, insisting on putting his name, the one word he could write, on every one.

At the end of the afternoon, Wendy Burroughs asked a question: 'What d'you say's gonna happen to all this, Miss?'

'Well, if I can get it all into my carriers, I'll take it home and make it into a big book. Really, you lot should do that, but I think we're running out of time. Mr Marriott won't want us behind in our work, or we won't get out of school again...'

'Warner'd never've let us out in the first place,' said Mamie Johnson, with authority.

Rachel went red. 'No need for that, Mamie. Anyway, I'll do the book at the week-end.'

'What d'yer want, working on a Saturday, Miss?'

'I'll enjoy it. Nice and peaceful without you lot around.'

'Won't you go to the dance, Miss?' asked Mary.

'The dance?'

'The club dance, every Saturday. Me mam never misses.'

'No. I don't dance,' Rachel replied. Elena was the one who danced. She was a natural, so they said at her classes. Rachel's wage was paying for the lessons.

'Don't dance?' said Mary, awe and contempt blending into the one question.

'My Mam's a brilliant dancer,' said Ian. 'She's won prizes, dancin'!'

'Your mam's a prossy, Ian. Everybody says.'

Ian dove across to attack her and Rachel pulled him back by his shirt. The bell clanged its way through the building, and they had to scramble to clear the desks and floor before the caretaker Mr Gomersall did his round at four. He expected 'his school' to be quite clear of the irritant of pupils and teachers as he embarked on a little gentle caretaking.

Ian stayed to the last, heaving chairs up onto

47

desks and generally helping Rachel to sort out. Watching him limp around, she frowned. 'Ian, I think I'd better come up with you and explain to your ... Nana about your foot, and going back to the doctor's.'

'She won't like it, Miss. She'll give me a clip.' His tone was quite resigned, business-like.

'Well, Ian, maybe a clip round the ear is a fair exchange for getting something done about that infection.'

They loaded the back of her van with carrier bags full of the afternoon's work, and chugged along, weaving backwards and forwards to avoid the holes and dips of the back streets.

Ian's house was closed; locked up.

'Now what?' said Rachel.

Ian had a key in his pocket, but he didn't want her going in the house with him and waiting. That'd earn him more than a clip on the ear. 'I'll wait. She's mebbe gone off somewhere. I'll just wait around here. She'll be back.' He shivered as a sharp wind cut down through the steep streets and right into the back of his shirt. He sounded bone tired.

'No. I can't just leave you, Ian. We'll go back to school and wait.'

The school was locked, its big doors weighed down with padlocks. Mr Gomersall was in Mr Warner's room, feet up, reading the *Evening Despatch*.

Rachel looked down at Ian, who was leaning against the wall, watching her. 'Right. You'll

48

have to come back with me. We'll get that leg cleaned up and then we'll go to the doctor ourselves.'

Sitting beside her in the van, he watched the route with interest as she drove out beyond the school and its square mile of streets, to a row of tall terraced houses overlooking the river. She made her way down a narrow entry at the side of one of the houses and parked the van in front of wide gates which opened onto a long garden.

He peered across the unkempt grass towards the dense cluster of trees and bushes at the far end. 'Them trees. Are they all yours?'

'Yes. Well, they belong to the garden and the garden belongs to the house.'

'And that caravan?'

It was at the very bottom of the garden, practically obscured by the trees. It was painted green and grey and rather battered: red and white checked curtains were drawn neatly across the windows.

'Yes,' she said.

'Is it for holidays?'

'No. Not since we were very little. My dad was keen on going out and about, before he died. He used to sit and read the papers in it on Sundays. Afterwards we used to play in it, here in the garden. My sister and I.' Those were the good times in this house, when their father's humour and sheer pigheadedness stopped their mother from becoming a Hitler in skirts. After

49

he died there had been no such constraints, and she got worse by the year.

Rachel undid the small gate in the fence and led the way to the back door, which was protected by an elaborate porch. Rachel's mother had always loved these tall houses. 'Very select. No riff-raff.' she had said, when they finally moved in.

Rachel wondered briefly about her mother's reaction to Ian. He would definitely come into her 'riff-raff' category. In the event, her mother just wrinkled her nose, making no objection to the boy having a bath, then being bundled into a big blue pullover belonging to Rachel's sister Elena.

The foot was a mess; the red stain from the infection creeping up his leg from the swollen ankle. Rachel bathed it in Dettol and dressed it with a broad dry bandage. All in all, she was pleased with her handiwork. Even her mother commented. 'I've always said soap and water makes all the difference. Costs next to nothing ... next to nothing ... these people...'

Ian sat still as the woman gazed at him through her thick-lensed glasses with their flyaway rims. He returned her look coldly, his light grey eyes moving from her permed grey head to her sensible shoes. She turned and walked angrily into the kitchen, slamming the door so the glass rattled.

He surveyed himself in the teak-framed hall mirror. He did look different. His hair, de-

50

greased and blown dry, was as light and fine as Sandra's. He had already made up his mind that when he was older he would dye it. Black, probably.

A girl with a ponytail, not much older than he was, was hanging round the bannister watching the proceedings. She grinned at him. 'You shall go to the ball!'

He scowled. Miss Waterman threw a bundle of socks at the girl and laughed. Ian looked on, his light eyes moving from one to the other. He thought again about Miss Waterman not being able to dance. His lip curled a little. At least Sandra could dance. He was pleased about that.

*   *   *

The doctor who dealt with him was small and neat, dressed in a three-piece suit that was just a touch too large. He smiled at Ian, then glanced across at Miss Waterman. 'Haven't seen you before. Are you new at the school? Here young feller, let's have a look at that.'

He peeled off the blue sock and the bandage, looked at the foot and scowled, then checked the card. 'Yes. We saw this before, didn't we?' He looked Ian in the eye. 'Been neglected since?'

Ian shrugged. The doctor turned to Rachel. 'I know they have a lot on their minds, those folks down there, but ...' He scribbled out a

51

prescription. 'Do you think you could just hang onto him for another hour, then I'll take him home and have a word with his—'

'Nana. It's his grandmother that you'll see,' she said mechanically.

'Right. I'll call for him at your house—the address?'

* * *

Back at the house, Rachel set Ian to work sorting out the carrier bags with the papers from the afternoon walk. She gave him all the pictures and rubbings to put into some kind of order,

She came to the piece of work labelled with Ian's own name. It was neat and carefully written, much of it copied in chunks from the book. She began to read; he had found a reference to a gibbet:

'On this spot, called The Old Cross, in 1527 was gibbeted the last person in this region. The evildoer was a boy who worked on the farm of a family called Trent. He killed the farmer's children most brutally, of the age seven, and three years. He persisted in saying he did the deed on the orders of Satan. The gibbet was a most cruel punishment, the boy staying alive for many days and his crys were so hard, so enduring, that people in cottages near moved away to get away from hearing them.'

Rachel's tension drew Ian's gaze and he watched her shiver slightly. 'Did you take all this from the book, Ian? It's ... carefully written.'

'Yes, Miss. I picked it cause of the cries. They can't spell it properly, like. But that's what it means, doesn't it?'

'What cries?'

'I told you. I could hear the boy howling. In that place.'

She shivered again.

His tone was very matter-of-fact as his head went down again over his task. 'Hey Miss! Look at this!' A rare excitement threaded into in his voice.

It was one of James Denton's rubbings.

She looked at it. 'Very nice, Ian.'

The black crayon and the white spaces thrown up by rubbing the crayon on the paper and the stone made an interesting negative. Then Ian turned his hand away from the window so that less light fell on the paper. She blinked.

In the half-light she could see a face. A young, round face.

'Can you see it, Miss, with its round mouth open? Couldn't we stick this beside my writing? So that could be the lad, howling. Like I told you.'

53

CHAPTER FOUR

PLAYING AROUND

Ian breathed a sigh of relief as he caught sight of his Nana's upswept hair through the net curtain. He cocked his head to one side to take in the full height of the man beside him.

'' 'S' all right, mister. They're home now.' He focussed hard at the broad side-planes of the man's face. His skin had a pinkish-blue sheen. He willed the man to go away. Go away. Sometimes it did work. Sometimes he could make things happen.

'That's all right, Ian. I just want a word with your mother ... your Nana.'

'No need, Mister. I can tell her.'

The man put his hand on Ian's shoulder, passing a thumb over the thin flesh. Ian wriggled under his tight grasp. His will, his concentration was not working on this man, with his three-piece suit, his antiseptic smell and his square strong hands.

'I'll tell her myself, Ian.'

The door squeaked as they went in. Mrs Sobell was standing framed in the doorway between the two rooms. The doctor frowned. He had been expecting an older woman. She was tall but quite small-boned; attractive in a way, with her fair hair tied back and upwards into a thick pony-tail. Her make-up was well-grained into her face; she was wearing a green shirt over a straight black skirt and high-heeled shoes.

He met her direct gaze.

'Who're you?'

'Grant. Doctor Grant—Mrs ...?'

'Sobell.' She rapped it out, glaring at him, ignoring his proffered hand.

'This will be your grandson?'

'This will be ... my daughter's son, if you like.'

'Well ... we were rather concerned about—'

'We?'

He reeled back at the whiplash delivery of the single word. Ian, standing between them, shuffled his feet. He felt sick.

'Well, it was noticed at school...'

'What was noticed? Who noticed it? That teacher?'

'It's the foot. Left unattended. It's infected now. It could be dangerous for Ian.'

'Was it that teacher? Miss Waterman?'

'Well, she did notice it. She's very concerned...'

'Nosy cow. Don't know how to keep her neb out of other people's affairs.'

'Nana!'

She reached out to crack Ian across his head. He ducked and the blow whistled through the air.

'Mrs Sobell, if I could just show you...'

55

Firmly the doctor placed Ian on a chair and peeled off the shoe and the sock. 'See that red stain? The infection is spreading. That stain shows just how far the infection is spreading. You'll have to keep it clean, and he'll have to take the medicine on the prescription. Or it'll spread further.'

She looked through the side of her face at the clean foot in its unfamiliar pale blue sock. 'Who put that poncy jumper on him? Them socks?'

'Well, Miss Waterman must've—'

'Teachers. Fucking teachers. Like little lasses, they are. Playing dolls with other people's kids. Can't be bothered to go the whole hog and get some of their own. Then they'd have to see what it was really like, the shitty nappies, the whining—'

'Mrs Sobell!'

Ian watched with interest as the doctor puffed up like some turkey-cocks he had once seen down the allotments. 'Will you see that this foot's kept clean, or do I have to call every day to check on it?'

'Nah, nah! I'll see it's clean, don't you worry. Can't have you calling every day, can I? Not a good-lookin' feller like you. They'll say I got a new man, won't they? The folks round here...'

Ian watched his Nana, suddenly all butter and honey, smiling up at the doctor, whose pinkish-blue cheeks had now turned purple. The man grabbed his bag, turned on his heel

56

and left without even looking again at Ian.

Shutting the door hard behind the doctor, Maureen Sobell leant on it and turned her head towards Ian. He stood there awkwardly, with one shoe off and one shoe on. Diddle-diddle dumpling...

'Now then little flower! Put new socks on you, did she? A new jumper? Where's your proper things?'

'They're in the bag.' He held up the carrier in front of him like a shield.

'Well, you'd better change back into them, hadn't you? Can't have you playing out in those good clothes, can we? Gotta keep them for best, for chapel, haven't we?'

Ian frowned. 'We don't go to chapel. Never have...'

'Change!' Her voice was chipped ice.

He flinched and tipped the contents of the carrier onto the table. Standing there in the stuffy kitchen he changed out of the soft clothes with their bright colours and into his own shirt and the socks which still retained their own independent shape, their own sour smell. He shivered.

Mrs Sobell folded the jumper and socks into a neat pile, smoothing and stroking them like a careful shopkeeper. 'There now, Ian. We'll just keep this lot for best, like. For when you go to chapel. Or wherever you go when you wear your best.'

He felt sick at the ominous sweetness in her

voice.

She went across to the cupboard beside the fireplace and tucked the pile of clothes into it with a great display of loving care.

She turned back to him, a thin smile on her lips. 'Now then, pet, you get yourself out to play. I've Mrs Fawcett to meet for the Bingo and our Sandra won't be back till late. Mind you play outside. Don't hang around the house causing trouble before nine o'clock.' Absently, she put the prescription behind the clock. 'It's a nice night. Real warm.'

She stayed there at the mantelpiece, tucking and pinning her ponytail up into a full bun at the back, using the small mirror propped up by the clock.

He watched her warily through the mirror. She whirled round. He flinched, but held his ground. You had to hold your ground with her.

'You heard! Play! Go out to play!' She pulled something out of the pocket of her black skirt, swinging her clenched fist in the air. He flinched again, then stood stock still as the fist came down. It stopped suddenly at the level of his eyes, then opened to reveal a medium size bar of fruit and nut chocolate. 'What about this, then? Knew I had something, didn't you? I got it at the shop for me and Mrs Fawcett at the Bingo. Here you are!' She shoved it into his rigid chest. 'Take it! You can tell that bloody teacher who can't even teach you proper, how

58

kind your Nana is to you, now, can't you? Spoiled rotten, that's what you are, spoiled rotten!'

Suddenly smiling, she gave him a hug, her arms like steel bands around his stiff body. 'Right! I'm off. Late already! We'll lock the door on our way out. Put your key under the stone as usual. Then you can go off and have a look out. A nice play. See your friends.'

In one minute he was outside the door, his nose wrinkling at the sticky hyacinth smell of her perfume. He put his hands into the pockets of his jeans, one hand still clutching the chocolate bar. Pursing his lips in a whistle, he set off down the street.

His feet seemed to lead their own way up through the back streets, quite deserted now. The Club and the Bingo drew people from their homes quite early on Wednesday evenings.

His feet walked him back to the Old Baths.

Looking up at the elaborate iron scrolls on the gate, it seemed a hundred days now since he had been there with James and Mamie and Miss Waterman. He tried to push the gate open, but he could not budge it. Miss Waterman had been strong, he thought, with those big hands of hers.

Kneeling down, he managed to squeeze under the wooden sleepers that were wedged against one side of the gate. In a second he was standing inside the stone enclosure which cupped the sky above in its two round stone walls.

The stones in the walls were bound together by clasping ivy and other creepers. The depression which had originally held the water for the great bath was still a rough square, although it was silted up with dead leaves.

He moved around, leaning down and cupping his hands around flowers which he had seen that afternoon. These same flowers were drawn and mounted, copied and labelled now, on Miss Waterman's sheets of paper. Here was coltsfoot with its stringy ropey stem and closed head, which they had first thought was a dandelion. The red dead-nettle with its soft green leaves, its purple flower hiding away and almost closed. A yellow flower like a buttercup, really called wild mustard. (Ian remembered Mary Charters' curly writing: '... also called charlock'. Charlock, charlock. He liked the word.) Then the lordly spikes of the rose bay willow herb flaring up out of the ground, silted up as it was with a widespread residue of leaf and leafmould, the ghosts and skeletons of past seasons.

Ian found a stone where he could sit on at the edge of the void. He sat there, his legs dangling down.

'Ian, hey, Ian!'

He looked across towards the barricaded gate. Two sets of eyes peered back through at him. 'What you want?' he growled, assuming a rough echo of Flicka Smith's voice.

'You'll get wrong, being in there. They'll get you...'

'They'll have to catch me first...'

The two little boys were muttering again together behind the gate. He couldn't hear their words. He didn't like not knowing what they said. 'Get yourselves in here, you two. It's great, a *brama* den, really good. You can climb through, down by the sleepers—on the side there.'

He felt like a bit of company now; someone to play with: he willed them to come. He knew if he willed it hard enough, they would come. It hadn't worked on the doctor, but he knew it would work on these two. They were much smaller than the doctor.

The conference on the other side of the gate continued. After a minute, two small figures scraped through under the sleepers. Ian knew them. Jonno and Michael, aged five and six, were half-brothers to Jimmy Denton. They both had rusty hair and freckles, but Michael, the younger one, was fairer and thinner. They wore neat T-shirts and shorts, a bit dusty with the day's use.

They were much smaller than Ian and had to look up at him as he jumped to his feet. He could see in his mind's eye how tall he must look to them. 'See? Isn't it a good den?' They looked up at him warily. He dipped into his pocket and pulled out the chocolate. 'Wanna bit?'

'Yeah!' They spoke in unison, their eyes glittering. Small sweaty hands palmed the chocolate into their mouths.

Ian pushed the remaining chocolate firmly back into the pocket of his jeans. 'Now we c'n play islands.'

'What's that?' said Jonno.

''S' easy. One of us is "on", and the others have to stay off the ground, like on islands. Everybody starts on an island. See, this bit of wall's an island...' He jumped onto a section of half-demolished wall. 'If you're "on" you count to ten, see? Then you can catch the others. Then when you're running between the islands you can get caught by the one who's "on". See? I'll be on first.'

The two boys moved from foot to foot, looking uncertainly at each other.

'Come on! It's great! We can have the rest of the chocolate after...'

This worked. The two of them clambered up onto crumbling high points, Michael having difficulty because of his short legs, which had still not quite shed their baby roundness.

'Now I count!' Ian started to count in a loud voice. '... now I come, ready or not!'

The game that followed was full of shouts and squeals from Michael and Jonno, yells and whistles from Ian. As he was so much bigger, he caught them quite easily. He had to slow down to let them catch him when they were on. He found it boring, being chased. He liked to

62

be the one doing the chasing.

One time, when Jonno was 'on', Ian lifted Michael onto a high section of walling, left like a pinnacle at the bottom end of the Baths.

Michael waited while Jonno counted carefully to ten, then looked round wildly. 'I can't get down! I can't get down!' he shrieked.

Ian, who had found his own high spot, jumped down and went across to look up at the little boy, who screamed, 'Get us down, Ian!'

Ian grinned up at him. 'Why should I?'

Michael started to cry. 'Gerrus down!' he shrieked.

'No. Jump!'

'Get him down, Ian.' Jonno came puffing across, and pulled at Ian's arm.

Ian flung the smaller boy away with some force, so that he sprawled on the ground. 'He's gotta jump. Jump, Mikey!'

Michael's breath was coming in great gasps. 'I'll fall!' he wailed.

'Jump!' Ian opened his arms.

The child shrieked again and leapt forward.

Ian caught him at the very last moment and set him lightly on the ground. 'There! Cry baby!'

He went across and pulled Jonno back to his feet. 'Now then, you two. What say we finish this chocolate?'

The sobs subsided.

All three of them made their way to the end of the Baths to sit on the stone wall with their legs dangling down into the pool space. Jonno and Michael sat very close together, eating the remaining chocolate in silence. When that was finished they clambered under the sleepers and stood together on the pavement outside.

'Right!' said Ian. 'We've got to meet here tomorrow, after school.'

Michael stuck out his bottom lip.

'We've got to!' said Ian. 'Haven't we, Jonno?'

Jonno looked down at Michael and up into Ian's light grey eyes. He moved fractionally away from his smaller brother. 'Will you have chocolate again?'

'Me Nana says I can have a giant bar.'

'A giant bar?'

'Yeah. I can make her get me anything. She goes on a bit, like. But I can still get anything.'

'Anything?'

'Anything. Right?'

'Right,' said Jonno at last. He set off to run, with Michael trailing after him.

Ian waited for a minute then set off in the same direction.

He stood at the corner of Michael and Jonno's street, watching the two of them vanish into their house. He hesitated at the corner of his own street. No use going home yet. It would be cold in there, and it was nowhere near nine o'clock. His Nana always checked. There would be bother if he hung round the house. She didn't like that.

He made his way to the edge of the town,

dawdling on, retracing the steps his whole class had taken that morning. All that laughing and working, all that walking, did seem a hundred days ago. He ploughed down the faintly marked path that they had walked in silence and came into the clearing where they had all stopped.

He sat down on the stone that James Denton had used so assiduously for his last stone-rubbing. Pulling the chocolate packet from his pocket, he smoothed out the silver with his tongue, picking up every last crumb of sweetness. His insides ached.

There was a rustle in the bushes. He jumped up as a boy emerged, heavier but not much taller than himself with a greasy thatch of fair hair.

'Whatcher want?' said Ian fiercely.

'Nowt. I was wonderin' what it were you wanted.'

The boy was thick-set, with rough trousers and a sleeveless jacket. Ian wrinkled his nose. 'You stink!'

'So d'you ... What's your name, then?'

Ian knew not to give his name. You never gave your name. 'What's your name yourself?'

'I'm called Pip Wales. I'm working on the farm.' He nodded down towards the west.

Ian stood up on the stone and craned his neck. He could just make out a cluster of low stone buildings, with smoke curling out of the chimneys. He heard the distant clatter and the shouting. 'What's it like working on a farm, then?'

'What's it like? It's like purgatory. Flogging yourself from morn till night. At everybody's beck and call. Even the little'ns. Six years old and givin' their orders.'

'You don't have to do what little'ns say.'

'I do. Or they tell on us, and I get the belt.'

Ian jumped down from the stone and glared at the boy. 'Lies. Fuckin' lies. Only a kid yourself.'

'I am about fourteen years. I've worked there five seasons.'

Ian frowned, feeling uneasy, like he sometimes felt around Tadger Smith. He jumped up and took another look down at the farm, now hazy in the wreath of its own smoke and the cool evening light. He turned around angrily to challenge the boy again.

He was gone. The bushes were still shivering from his hasty exit. Ian turned back again, and the farm was gone, veiled entirely by a slice of dark. All he could see were green fields and the illuminated ribbon of the new by-pass road.

CHAPTER FIVE

FAMILY LIFE

When Ian got home, yellow light was glimmering through the wavy crack in the red curtains. A loud whistle of relief forced its way across his tongue. She was in then. That meant he could go in himself.

She didn't like him being in there on his own. 'See to yourself better outside, son, shan't you? In here you'd be up to something, rooting around and breaking things. You know what you're like.'

Ian did know what he was like. He didn't really blame her for wanting him outside. Things had happened in the house.

That time he was four-and-a-half, in on his own, he had set fire to the kitchen, trying to light the grill to make some toast. Rescued by neighbours. She'd given him a real good belting for that. He had to miss school for the next two days because of the bruises.

Then that time he was six, one night when Maureen was at the Bingo, he had taken all the packets and bottles out of the kitchen cupboard and mixed them together in a delightful cement on the floor of the front room. On her new sheepskin rug as well.

Then when he was seven there had been the

67

other fire, so bad they'd had to move house. Then there was the flood last January.

He didn't really blame his Nana. The ban was fair enough, when you thought about it.

She was in the back kitchen.

He put his head round the door.

'There you are, bonny lad!'

Friends! He grinned with relief.

'Wondered where you'd got to. Wherever you been? Your tea's nearly ready.'

'I was messing about, like. Up near the Old Baths.'

'You want to keep away from there. Dangerous bloody place. Bloody council ought to see to it, sitting on their fat arses...' She cracked two eggs into the big frying pan, and poured boiling water onto two tea-bags. 'There, it's just about ready. If you're anything like me, son, you're famished. That Bingo really makes you feel hungry, don't it?'

'D'ya get a win?'

'I was waiting for one number for a house three times. Had a line up, though.'

'How much?'

'Eight pounds. Split between me and Mrs Fawcett; that's four quid each. Just about covers your costs really. But you've got to have a bit of fun, ain't yer?'

'Yes, Nan.' He was hungry and weary. Half past nine was late for tea, even in this house.

'You sound all in, pet. That bloody teacher of yours, and her doctor friend racing you all over the place. Always keen to interfere, ain't they?'

'Yes, Nan!' He wished that she'd get the chips onto the plate.

'Your poor old foot still hurtin'?'

He realised that it was. 'A bit.'

'Well, I'll be down at that chemist to get your medicine, first thing. You can count on it, pet. Lucky I got that win, isn't it? Have to pay through the nose for everything now, haven't you?'

He knew there was nothing to pay. No charge for children. She always liked to egg up a favour. 'Yes, Nan.'

The chips were on the plate now. He sat opposite her at the kitchen table and started to pick up the chips with his fingers. The salty potato tasted delicious as he bit through the crisp skin. His whole body responded to the oily fluffy taste of the chip; the ache started to recede from his diaphragm.

Maureen sat down and set about her chips with a fork. She looked across at him. 'Like that teacher, do you?' she said with her mouth full.

'She's alright, Nan; doesn't get onto you, like. We've been doin' this thing about places round here. We went this walk...'

'Walking? She wants something to do, doesn't she? Walking? And there you are with your bad foot...' She packed bread and chip and egg onto a fork, then bit into it with some

69

satisfaction. '… She should be doing proper work … sums … making you do proper work so you don't end up in that class for thickies, and then on to the dole like the other idle sods round here.'

'But it was all right, what we did, Nan!'

'Yes! Bloody marvellous doing nowt. Call it schooling?'

'You learn—'

She was not listening. Stabbing away at her chips, she was thinking about her own school just after the war. No outings then. At your desks. Head down. Mental arithmetic, tables, spelling three times a week; the teacher belting you across the head if you breathed loud. Then, when you were older, nicking off single lessons; then whole days, spending the time you won in cafes in the town. She smiled. 'Happiest day of my life when I left school proper.' She said this out loud.

'That's cos you didn't like it Nana. Miss Waterman, she makes it OK … doesn't even get onto you about noise.'

'Miss? Miss? She's only a bloody kid herself. Dossed down in a feather bed … don't know how many beans make five. Coming here, thinking she knows…'

Ian was carefully constructing a chip sandwich, cocking an absent ear to what she was saying. He liked it when she sat and talked to him, no matter what the topic, no matter who she was doing down.

70

She looked across at him. Granted he needed a bit of a wash now, but just sometimes he looked so like his mother, like Sandra, even if it did sit funny on him, him being a boy. Sandra had been such a pretty little thing. Wide blue eyes, pale skin, natural white hair. Attention wherever she went. She got a lot of attention.

There had been that problem, of course, when she'd got that bit too much attention when she was fifteen, falling wrong with Ian like that. Only good thing was she'd been careful since. No more unwanted bundles.

'Nan? Are there any more chips?'

'No. Have some more bread.'

'Nan?'

She was turning the pages of the *Daily Mirror*, which was laid out beside her plate. 'What now?' She didn't look at him.

'That chocolate was great.'

'Chocolate? Oh that! Just you remember, that chocolate should've been for me and Mrs Fawcett at the Bingo.'

'I saw Terry Lawson down the rec. and he made me give him a piece. I said I'd got it off you, but he wouldn't believe me. Said I'd nicked it.'

'Cheeky bugger. Who's he to say?'

'Well, he said you never gave me anything.'

'Cheeky bugger!' she repeated, turning another page of her paper.

'Well, anyway, I said you'd won in Bingo

71

and that you'd buy a giant bar for us.'

She reached out her hand and landed him a clip over the ear. His head rang.

Her eyes were still on the paper. 'Trouble with you, Ian Sobell, is you think your Nana was born yesterday. Never even saw that Terry Lawson, did you? You just think you can screw chocolate out of me, don't you? Lyin's a sin, you know. And you'll burn in hell for it.'

The good feeling from the Bingo had drained from her. She looked angrily at the smudged face opposite. Tumult! Tumult he'd brought into their lives. Sandra and her. He was a funny enough kid. He could make you laugh sometimes. He could be quite a clown. But what a tie! Kids were always a tie. 'Time you were in bed, past time really. Our Sandra'll be in soon and she won't want you around after a hard night's work.'

Her voice faded. Her eyes returned to her paper. Ian went through into the front room and stood still. He heard the teapot rattle as she poured herself another cup of tea, then the low hum of the television.

Very delicately, using both hands, he opened first her handbag, then her purse. He extracted two pounds and held them tight in his hand. 'Night, Nan.'

There was no response from the kitchen.

On his way to his capsule of a bedroom, he pushed open the door to Sandra's room. The street light shone down like grey gauze onto the neat single bed with its pink quilt and white velvet headboard.

He pushed the door open further. The light from the landing slid in, wiping out the grey-gauze evening light, replacing it with a yellow glow. The walls of the room were dark pink, shading in with the nice pink carpet and contrasting with the white sheepskin rug.

He moved across to the long dressing table and looked at himself through Sandra's mirror. He passed his hand across the bottles and jars with a magician's wave. One bottle, clear glass, had a golden stopper which was decorated with a garland of golden ivy. He picked up the bottle and sprayed a fine suspension of perfume into the air. In the borrowed light he could see the droplets suspended there for a long time, and was careful not to let them drop on any part of himself. He breathed the sweet smell in, closing his eyes.

Now Sandra was there for him, her long hair combed down, wearing one of the light-coloured dresses she wore for work. Now she was there again, this time in her ponytail and jeans, carrying a full carrier-bag, ready to take him on a bus-ride to the sea.

Normally Ian didn't see too much of Sandra. He didn't see enough of her. She slept all morning and went off early in the afternoon. She came back very late, often when he was in bed. Sometimes she didn't come back at all.

When she was there, Ian often felt invisible. She would gaze right over or through him as she carried on a conversation with her mother. Sometimes he would play a game, dodging into her eyeline, making her move her gaze, until she cried in exasperation, 'Ian, will you stop dodging around like that?'

Then he was satisfied. He had made her see him.

Sometimes—he had never been able to work out exactly why—she would pull him to her, her soft hands hard, her slender clasp too strong. Then he would stand quite still, not quite knowing how to respond. One time he had kissed the soft cheek that was so close to him. She had pushed him away, laughing. 'Why, who's a sloppy boy, then? You don't kiss your Mam like that!'

So after that, when she held him, he had just stood very still.

Now, putting the gold-topped scent bottle back onto the dressing table, he eased open the right hand drawer. He pulled out the black pottery cat with the red ribbon; the one he had bought for Sandra last year for her birthday, from the school jumble sale. Once the fuss was over, he had never seen it around again. He knew that she kept it here, though. Among her tights and talcum powder. He had discovered it in one of his regular searches. It had pleased him to know it was there, that it hadn't gone out to the bin with other rubbish in one of her

74

regular clear-outs.

His grandmother's voice rang out from down below. 'Ian! Are you in bed yet?'

He flew into his own bedroom. This was darker, with no enlivening pink, no soft white rug. He stripped off to his underpants. His bandaged foot glowed out at him, white in the darkness. He pulled back the blankets and jumped into his bed. It was still damp from the night before, so he settled down to wait for his body heat to warm it up.

As he waited for this to happen, he squeezed hard on the two pounds he had taken from his Nana's purse.

He did not cry. It was, really, a long time since he had needed to cry.

*   *   *

Rachel sat back from the table and stretched. The book of the walk had come together very well. She had added her own commentary at the front and straightened up the children's printing here and there.

The door rattled and her mother came in, a cup of tea in her hand. 'You might as well have it up here if you're staying up here all night,' she said gracelessly.

Rachel was used to her mother's accusing tone, used without fear or favour to everyone: the grocer, the window cleaner or her own two daughters; more especially Rachel. It was a lifetime's habit cultivated in a marriage to a man she neither liked nor respected but had once deemed suitable.

Rachel took the cup from her and placed it carefully on the table. 'Thank you mother,' she said. She knew full well the apparent kindness of the cup of tea was an excuse for her mother to enter her room.

'Can't think why you stay up here all night,' her mother sniffed. 'Me stuck down there. Our Elena still out enjoying herself.'

Good for Elena. At least she knew *how* to enjoy herself. 'It is my room, and I had work to do,' said Rachel carefully.

'You could work in the dining room.'

'I want to work in here, in my own space.'

Her mother glanced round. 'Can't think why. It's a tip.'

'So it is. I like it that way.'

When Rachel had finally come home from college the previous summer, her room had been transformed: stripped out, everything painted white, even the furniture. Apart from a token book of poems by her bedside all her books and records had gone, packed away into cases in the loft.

The old, mild Rachel would have accepted that. But bringing in a wage was beginning to make her feel less vulnerable to her mother's cold rages, and she had started to rebel. The books and records were all back now, standing around in drunken piles and stacked on a set of

76

shelves she had constructed herself from planks and rough bricks. The ghastly white furniture was draped in cloth and shawls. The walls were covered with posters from her college room, of Che Guevera and Buddy Holly.

'Can I get on now, Mother?'

'That dreadful smelly child, Rachel. You made a big mistake there.'

'I had to do that for him. There was nothing else to do.'

'It's not your problem.'

'It *is* my problem. I have to face it every day.' She squared up a pile of exercise books. 'Now, can I get on?'

Mrs Waterman stared at her daughter, her glasses glittering. 'It's bringing out the worst in you, that school, those children, no mistake.'

Rachel stood up and held the door for her. 'Perhaps it's bringing out the best in me. You never know.'

She banged the door behind her mother, and went to put a record on her record player. She turned it up loud and sat drinking her tea, imagining her mother cringing at the sound of Fats Domino's voice. '*I found my thrill. On Blueberry Hill. I found my thrill ... when I met you...*'

She wondered briefly if there had ever been any romance or passion in her parents' lives together. There had certainly been no evidence of it while she and Elena had been around. Her mother had an absolute revulsion for anything sexual. Perhaps they had only ever done the act twice. Like the biblical "begetting". Once to beget her, and once to beget Elena. She sighed. Poor Dad.

*   *   *

The heavy door of the car slipped from Sandra's hand and closed with a very solid thump.

She watched the car purr away down the narrow, barely-lit street. Only two houses still showed lights. Generally around here, people lived their lives early—early to bed; early up and out for work on the seven-thirty shift at Clarkson's Domestics; early to the club for a front table, then early home to get sorted for the next day.

One or two sets of curtains had twitched as the car had slid to a stop, but usually even that sound was registered as routine, like the routine judgement always accorded to Sandra herself.

She let herself in with her key. Maureen was still up, already pouring boiling water onto the tea-bags. 'Cup of tea, love?'

'Great, Mam.'

Sandra eased off her high sandals and stretched out her legs in front of her, wriggling her toes towards the gas fire.

Maureen brought in the tray, carrying the

china cup and saucer for Sandra, the mug for herself. 'You look tired, love.'

'On since three o'clock till now's no joke.'

Maureen was proud of Sandra doing a job that wasn't ordinary. Her official job mainly involved serving and clearing drinks in that club and talking to people. In the evening she sang a little with the resident local band. Then there were the other things that Maureen chose not to think about.

Sandra had always had a good voice. Maureen had worked scrubbing out the bank to send her for lessons. Now, being on show so much for her job, Sandra always had to look immaculate. She always took at least one change of clothes to work with her. Maureen loved Sandra's clothes, and took good care of them.

All things considered, Maureen was pleased about Sandra's job. And it was well-paid compared with the factory shifts, the house-slaving, or the dole, enjoyed now by the girls who had sat alongside her at school.

Even so, once Sandra had paid for the calibre of clothes and make-up that Eddie Bayers approved of, and the taxis home when she wasn't favoured with a lift, there was as little left as if she had worked in a factory.

'Did you get to sing?' asked Maureen.

'Yeah. Three spots,' said Sandra wearily.

'You never know, pet. You never know!' Maureen dreamed that Sandra would be 'discovered' and move on and up. Even to the telly.

'No chance!' Sandra looked across at her mother with an insight born out of exhaustion from her own weary routine. 'You've got it wrong Ma. I keep saying. There's no glamour.'

Maureen clashed her mug back onto the tray, spilling some tea. She lived through the day for these few moments of glamour, turned over and raked through like second hand clothes: Sandra meeting people whose names were in the local press; Sandra swaying and singing routine classic popular songs in a single spotlight.

'Mam, I'm just part of the wallpaper there. Just part of the fixtures and fittings. I'm twenty-seven now. Have to watch meself like a hawk. Younger birds are there to catch Bayers' eye. Fifteen, sixteen years old. Some even have good voices.'

Her dreams dismissed, Maureen's hand shook slightly as she grasped the tray, her lips going to a thin line. 'Whole lot of trouble with your Ian today.'

Sandra sighed. 'What's up now?'

'You know that foot he hurt—last week was it? Well, that cow of a teacher poked her nose in again. Took him to the doctor. Took him to her bloody house! Put him in the bath—the bath, mind you—and put a whole lot of different clothes on him!' Maureen went across to the cupboard and raked out the clothes. Pale blue. Soft materials. 'See? Cheeky cow! Then she sent this doctor across with him when I got home. Threatened me, he did!'

Sandra sat up straight. 'Threatened you?'

'Said he'd come back every day to check.'

'Check what?'

'That I'd gone for the medicine and was giving it to our Ian. He said the foot was infected.'

Sandra lay back again on the soft chair. 'Well, you'll just have to make sure you do that, won't you? That's what you get the money for.' Another part of her heavy expenses. Ian was Maureen's job.

'Me, I think you'd better do something yourself about that nosey cow of a teacher. Isn't even your age. And she thinks she knows everything. Thinks we're muck. She knows nowt.'

'Do something, then.'

'Do something yourself. He's your kid not mine. Tell her to keep her bloody nose out. Tell her what a handful he is. How you have to keep on top of him, not encourage him.' Maureen pulled a pad out of a drawer.

Sandra closed her eyes, and pressed her head against the back of her chair. The spun glass of her hair reflected in its shiny green threads.

'Tell her,' said Maureen firmly, putting the pad in one hand, and a pen in the other. 'Tell her what a little bugger he really is. Tell her about the fire. And the flood.'

Sandra sat up and started to write with the pad on her knees. The biro sat awkwardly in her hand because of the long fingernails.

Watching her, Maureen though how different it would have been if Ian had been a girl. You got something out of a girl. It would have been fun dressing a girl again, and showing her how to go on. All a boy could do was grow up into a man.

*　　*　　*

Ian didn't want to take the note to school. Maureen insisted. 'You have to. Sandra wrote it specially, before she went to bed. Specially.'

'What's it say?'

'It's none of your business.'

'I'm not taking it.'

Her hand winged down, too fast for him to duck. It stung his cheek and forced his head to one side. He didn't cry, although his nose itched with the pain.

'I told you before, Ian Sobell. You do as you're told. No ifs and buts.'

He stuffed the letter into the back pocket of his jeans and looked up at her, blinking the wet out of his eyes. 'Nana—that thing about Terry Lawson. It was right, you know. Can't I have some money for that chocolate?'

Her hand went to her bag on the mantelpiece. He held his breath. She would find that the money was missing and he'd really

82

get a belting. Playing at risk like this was one of his games. Like jumping on the 'horse' in front of Flicka Smith and causing that mayhem. Now he had dared himself that his Nana wouldn't go for her bag. And here she was, softening. What was the matter with her?

Her hand moved away from the bag and he breathed a sigh of relief.

She scowled at him. 'True or not, what makes you think your Nana has that kind of money? Now get yourself to school. And don't you have no truck with that bloody teacher. She'll get you into trouble. See if I'm right! You see!'

CHAPTER SIX

ISLANDS

'Miss, have you still got that book? Can I have a look at it?'

Rachel looked down at Ian's narrow face. His eyes were shadowed. That pink mark on his cheekbone looked like the blooming of a bruise; not unusual for him or for others in the class. She had asked about it in the staffroom and they'd told her she could report it, but she had to realise that these children lived like that. They were used to it, in those families.

Apart from the bruise, Ian was his familiar

self, thin legs clad in greasy jeans. Today, though, they were topped by a clean shirt.

It was morning break. The classroom was empty apart from the two of them. 'What happened to those clothes? The ones I gave you, Ian?'

'Oh, those . . .' he said. His pale eyes looked into hers. 'I got a note for you . . . Sandra—that's my mam, really—she wrote it last night. When she got in from work. My Nana got her to. She writes all our letters for us.' Ian handed her a battered envelope.

It was written in a round schoolgirlish hand:

'Dear miss you have no need taking my Ian off like that and putting fancy clothes on him. he is a bad lad and tears his clothes and needs strong clothes. he is wicked and wets the bed on purpose just to give his poor Nan some more work he lies and needs punished. he doesn't need your poncy clothes so I have given them a poor kid who needs them. Stop messing him about. Leave him alone. Just teach him his letters and numbers yours faithfully Sandra Sobell.'

Ian watched the bony, open face become cold and pinched. She glared down at Ian, who was staring at her. She stared back at him.

'Miss?'

'Yes?' She voice was hoarse. Her face was red. The thing she liked least in life was to be embarrassed.

'Can I look at that book again, Miss? That history book?'

'What history book?'

'You know. The one about the old crossroads.'

Blindly, she reached a hand to a high shelf behind her and found the book by feel, by its size and its loose binding. 'Why do you want it?'

'Well, I was up there last night again. At the crossroads. I walked up. An' I think I saw that lad. You know. That lad?'

'Lad?'

'Yeah. That lad who howled. And the farm as well. Then it was dark and I couldn't see it again. Then I seen him again. Just.'

She slipped down from the desk pedestal and sat down on the edge of the dais, pulling him down beside her. 'Tell me what happened.'

He told her all about his evening, although he missed out the details of the game he played with Michael and Jonno.

'... Then I saw this lad. Talked to him like you here. Honest, Miss.'

She put an arm round his narrow shoulder and pulled him to her. 'You've been dreaming, Ian. You lay down on that clearing, and dropped off. The infection in your foot would have made you sleepy.'

'But, Miss, I tell you—'

The door clattered open and Jack Marriot

came roaring in. He stopped as he saw her sitting on the edge of the dais. His voice moderated. 'What's this, Miss Waterman? Fraternising with the enemy?'

Rachel and Ian, crouched near the floor as they were, froze, thief-handed. Then Ian flew out from under Rachel's protective arm and ducked through the open door, dodging Jack Marriot's reaching hand.

The big man looked down at Rachel, then pulled her up from her low perch, keeping his thick hand on her wrist. 'I would watch that, if I were you, Miss Waterman. Never know where it might lead. Kids like these.'

She wrenched her arm out of his grasp and looked him in the eye, her tight jaw strangling her voice as it came out. 'The day I see the kids as the enemy, *Mister* Marriot, I'll be out of this so-called profession like a shot.'

He chuckled softly at this. 'Don't think we haven't all said some such thing at one time or another, little Rachel. But here you find us, toiling away, still behind the enemy lines. Right down from holy-roller Warner, through mean old Marriot, even now to rosy-cheeked, starry-eyed Rachel Waterman!'

'Oh!' She barged past him, then slowed down and made her way to the staffroom, her anger at the letter seeping back into her.

At the end of break she returned to the classroom to find Ian with his head buried in the old book. He did not look up as she called, with more force than usual, for order in the classroom.

Jane Brown, in the front at the right, jumped at the surprise of Miss Waterman bellowing like that, and shook her head. Rachel caught her reaction and made her stand at the front, face to the wall, for insolence.

*   *   *

After school, back at the Old Baths, Ian set about enhancing his game. He worked away, building new islands from the broken stone which had collapsed into the nettles and the rose bay willow herb. Some stones were so large he could only drag them or corner-walk them to their new places. He made one particularly high pile on top of an existing wall. For this he had to clamber up, clutching heavy stones which scratched his hands.

The air was heavy with early evening heat. Sweat dropped from his brow onto his arms as he worked. His hands were white-patched with nettle stings; his fingers were sore, their bitten ends bleeding.

The job completed, he played his own game of islands: running, jumping with a rocking balance onto piles in every part of the space. Some piles were precarious; he teetered perilously as he stood on them. To solve this problem, he stuffed the cracks with loose earth. This he converted to sticky mud with water scooped from the river which bordered the bottom wall of the Old Baths.

Finally, he stood beside the gate, surveying the results of his labour It was good. Just the right amount of space between the islands, which were now really high. He sat on the highest island and waited, willing them to come.

He pulled the bar of chocolate from his pocket and lay it on the stone wall beside him. It had softened in the heat of his exertions, moulding itself a little to the shape of his thigh.

He looked at its lumpish shape and felt angry. Its neat, hard edges, its clear silver shape, had dissolved into a rounded thin lump. Moving it about on a flat stone, he pressed it with his hot muddy hand to straighten it. It did become more or less straight, although it still looked used and dirty. He banged the flat stone beside the chocolate with his fist, his anger dissolving in the way it stung and hurt by his own exertions.

Then he waited quite patiently.

It was after six when they came, creeping under the bottom sleeper at the gate. Jonno came first, pulling an unwilling Michael behind him. He looked across and up towards Ian.

'Now Ian!'

'Now, Jonno! Now Michael! You in on this game?'

'Yeah,' said Jonno. 'But we've gotta get home for our tea, after.'

They approached him, where he sat on his pinnacle. Michael hovered just a bit behind Jonno.

'What about this, then? Didn't I tell you my Nana would get a big bar for me?' He grabbed the battered chocolate from the stone beside him and jumped lightly down to ground level.

Jonno whooped and Michael grinned, showing his baby teeth. The three heads went together over the chocolate.

'Looks like it's been through a crusher,' said Jonno.

'D'yer not want any, like?' said Ian.

'Yeah!' They breathed the word, one after another.

Flourishing his arm like a magician, Ian broke off a strip of three squares for each of them. Michael was in such a hurry to stuff his into his mouth that it spread in a sticky stain all over the lower part of his face.

Ian started to play, step-up, step-down, onto a large loose stone. It wobbled and rocked under his feet.

'Now! Let's play!'

'What're we playing?' asked Michael.

'Remember? Can't you remember? Islands. We played it yesterday.' He raced right across the open space. 'Only I've made more islands, see?'

'Great, Ian, Great!' Jonno breathed appreciatively.

'We'll fall down...' started Michael.

'Don't be a bloody idiot,' said Ian, 'Just a bloody baby, isn't he, Jonno?'

'Yeah. Just a baby.'

Michael stood quiet now.

'The game's a bit different, now. Cause I've built all these special islands for us, haven't I? So now you can only stay on one island once. So everybody has to jump on every island. See?'

Michael was looking round uncertainly. Jonno was grinning. 'Sounds alright,' he said.

'Shall we do "Dibs" for "man"?' said Ian.

'Do "Dibs",' said Michael.

They did the play with fists. Michael was 'man'.

The game was fast and full of tumbles; noisy shrieks pierced the still air. The increased number of islands improved the game. There was more scrambling, more catching. One or two of Ian's islands crumbled under the assault and three of them worked together to rebuild them.

Ian was content. This is my place, he thought. My place.

After half an hour they finally collapsed and went to lean against the outside wall, gasping for breath.

'More chocolate.' said Michael.

Ian pushed the battered pack firmly back into his pocket. 'Nah. I'm saving it.'

'What for?'

'For Sunday afternoon.' He knew his Nana

would be out then, on what she called her errands. 'Three o'clock. You can tell the time, can't you?'

'Yeah,' said Michael.

'Bet you can't!'

'I can,' said Jonno.

Ian had his doubts. But then he smiled. 'Right! Listen! When the big hand is on the twelve and the small hand's on the three. Three o'clock. Come out then.'

Jonno was relieved. He wasn't always absolutely sure of the clock. Some days it seemed as though he could do it. Sometimes it made no sense at all.

'Both of you, mind! Make sure Mikey comes! Only works with three.'

'Right!' said Jonno.

'Right!' said Michael. 'It was great today, great!'

'Now we've gotta go,' said Ian decisively, 'your Mam'll have your teas ready.'

The three of them wriggled out under the planks one after the other. The best of friends, they moved out into the hot night.

*　　*　　*

This time after the game, Ian made his way straight back up to the crossroads. Standing on the stone, he strained around in the growing gloom to catch sight again of the farm. He screwed up his eyes and looked really hard and

91

put his will upon it. Then he smiled as he began to hear the farming sounds and he smelled the woodsmoke. Then, finally, he could make out the low roof and the chimney through the early evening mist.

'I knew tha'd be back.'

He whirled round. The boy was making his way down the path that Ian had used. He was swishing his stick from side to side against the bushes. Ian could see the twigs as they floated down from their parent branch, broken by the boy's slashing action.

The boy stood at the opposite side of the clearing, bringing the stick up so he was holding it in two hands. Ian stood stock still on his high point, looking down at the boy, the rough thatch of fair hair, the round face.

'I willed tha back. I knew tha'd be back.'

Ian knew about this willing people to do things. Couldn't he do that himself? He stood stiff and wary on his stone. 'Why'd you come back here then? Why get me back here then?' He could hear his own voice, thin and reedy, like the whistling of a bird.

'Cos I knew thoo'd listen. I knew thoo'd listen. Sit down. Sit tha down.'

The little clearing was suddenly hot, unbearably hot. Ian could feel the sweat pouring down his back from his shoulders. He opened his mouth wide to pull in some air, some breath. 'I'll sit down only if you sit down where you are,' he gasped, putting the strength

92

of his will against that of this round-headed boy.

'I c'n do that.' The boy sat down where he was and leaned back into a bush so that he was entirely surrounded by bright green May leaves. 'Now first. Tell us tha name.'

Clambering down to sit on the stone gave Ian a moment to think. He knew that you must not give your name. 'Nah. Can't do that. Not allowed. Go on. You talk.'

'Well charver, it started with a game and ended with a death. Now that's a rare cruelty game in itself. No, charver, don't leap up. Sit thee and listen...'

CHAPTER SEVEN

PIP WALES

'They came over when I had just reached the last woodstack, see?'

'Who did?' Ian wriggled to settle his bottom into a more comfortable position on the stone. The strong heat had gone. It was cooler. He would sit, just sit and listen. Nothing to be frightened of here. Nothing spoiling, as his Nana would have said.

Pip Wales rubbed his palm across his mouth. 'Littl'ns belonging to this farmer-feller I worked for. Reuben his name; other name

93

Trent. He never liked me to stop while there was a scrap of daylight left. That made summers really hard, see? Always sommat to do. Worse'n the winters, funny enough.'

His voice was coming and going, sometimes loud, sometimes faint and distant.

'Anyway, one job that week, on top of the usual, was building the woodstacks for the winter. I'd dragged wood from all over the farm and the backcountry. Made three big stacks of kindling all told. Lots of coppicing around, them times'

'Coppicing?' said Ian.

'Branches of big old trees that sprout again the next year.'

Pip's voice was stronger now.

'Well, I'd just finished choppin' and stackin' the second stack and I'm just standin' there wipin' the sweat out of my eyes. Them two—'

'Who?' said Ian?

'Kinder belonging the farmer. Anyway they had climbed up the wall, and were kinda leanin' ower the top, see? I took no notice of 'em, just balanced a chock of wood and took a swing with the axe. But then, like, it twisted back off the chock and wrenched me arm, see? Axe was blunt, even though I'd sharpened it just an hour gone. Work it'd done, see? Made it blunt. Mebbe like me . . . too worn out to work. Right thing to do, been to sharpen it there and then. But I was tired, see, like no animal is ever tired.

94

'Well, I threw the axe down and picked up the bit of wood that's turned it off and looked at it, smelled it, real close. It was quick wood— lightnin' wood. Struck by lightnin' and dead as a doornail. D'you know about quick wood? Kind of soapy in colour and no weight to it?'

Ian shook his head. He knew nothing about trees or leaves, or wood.

'By rights, the axe should'a blasted it to pieces, but it turned the axe off. Funny, that. Then the older one, Janey, of the littl'ns belonging to the farmer, she shout over. "What you got there, Pip?" she says ... She has this rasping voice, see? Like all the Trents. Better listen to birds, even the mooin' cow, any day, than listen to the raspin voices of them Trents.

'The other of'm, called Madoc, just sits beside her, grinnin', grinnin' away. Then he shouts across, "Well, what you got? Soft fool. Soft fool. Idiot-lad. Idiot-lad." He goes on shoutin' that ... those words...

'"It's touchwood, quickwood," I say, just to shut him up.

'"Touchwood? Quickwood?" says Janey, that rasping voice echoin' my words ... They often make an echo of what I say, the way I say things, but make it sound, like gormless, see? Then they shout "Gippo!" all the time.

'"What's it do?" she shouts. "Show us, Gippo. Go on! Show us."

'"It's magic," I say. "Wood struck by lightning; all dead in a second. Tha can mek a smoke wheel out of it and mek the ghost of the tree sing."

'"Gippo stuff," she says. "You'll have to show us now, else it's more gippo lies."

'Now I was real feared of them, these little'ns. But I tell you, charver, I was more feared of their Da. So I say, "I have to chop this last stack by dark or your Da'll get onto us."

'"Show us! Show us!" they chant, jumping off the wall, comin' real close. I shy off like some hoss. They know I like nobody too near me. They press, press right in. They get hold of me by the arms, pull me down, see? I swing round, right round, to throw them off. Too close they are, too close.

'Young Madoc, he starts this shriek: "Da! Da! That Pip's hittin' us again!" Now, I never hit'm ever, see? I never hit anybody, never even a dog or a hoss. They, like, they got into this way of sayin' that thing all the time to get round Reuben. Then he would belt me, tan me with the whip he used for his hoss. Marks'd stay on me for weeks ... I can tell you, I soon got into the way of doing what they said, young as they were. They knew how to mek us.

'"Da! That Pip's gettin our Madoc!" shrieks Janey now, her eyes, like, shining like a beacon.'

Ian frowned, concentrating harder. Inside the deep tones of Pip Wales, Ian could hear, like a radio on the borderline between two stations, the high piping voices of much

96

younger children. Followed by Pip's own rough deep tones.

'"Shut up! Shut that!" I tell these charvers ... I'm desperate now. They wail on ...

'"Shut up!" I say, my flesh creepin' at the thought of that Reuben. "Shut up and I'll show you about the touchwood, down at the Three Spike. Down by the barn."

'Now, charver, Three Spike is this field by the river, see. It was down there where I saw you that first time. And all them other charvers. A barn there—three sides of an old house, and bits of its roof. Reuben kept extra feed down there, for the beasts at that end.

'Those littl'ns, then, they shut up. Looked at me, cold, like.

'I say, earnest, like to them, "I'll show you, honest, soon as I've finished this stack," says I.

'They've got me going now, them charvers. I'm thinkin' about the last time they told the lies about me hittin' 'em. Reuben belted me so hard I couldn't breathe nor walk for a full week.

'"Alright," says Janey, smiling at me real sweet. "When you've finished the stack, you show us. Or else we'll ..."

'I swung real hard at that last stack, thinking on that them charvers've lost me another hour from my sleep. Sleep bein' the only time I could get away from any of 'm, see?

'The wood cracked like the driest kindling. Sometimes, I tell thee, I feel really strong, like I

97

could crack the world right open, like the world was a banty egg. See?'

Pip Wales looked across at Ian, deepest brown eyes gazing into lightest grey. 'You listenin', charver?'

Ian crouched lower on his stone opposite the boy in his halo of green leaves, giving him look for look. 'I'm listenin'. Yes I am.'

'Well, it was no time 'fore I got down to Three Spike. At first—no sign of 'em. Soon enough though, a stone flew and cut my cheek. Another raised dust to add to the layers on my boots. Those two little'ns, they were sittin' inside the loft on heaps of hay. They kicked away and it floated in wisps through the air, landing and sticking on their clothes, in their hair. There were wisps of it on my jerkin. On my hair.

'"Come up here, Pippo, Gippo! And show us your magic wood," calls Janey, peering down. "Come up here..."

'"Na!" says I, "We'll be making fire. Smoke wheels. Could burn that lot down."

'They scramble down. Janey brushes some hay wisps off her pinny, those bright eyes staring, staring at me. Then she rasps out, her voice just like her Da's, "Now, Gippo, show us this magic wood, this smoke wheel."

'Well, the lumps of wood come out of my pocket and onto the ground. Then I get me knife, which I always keep sharp, like. Then me tinder. Always dry, that.'

98

'Tinder?' said Ian. 'What's that?'

'You make fire with it. It makes fire.' said Pip Wales, his tone indifferent, wanting to get on.

' "You need a piece of wood this size, see?" I says to those two, cutting off a chunk the size of my fist with my knife. I smooth it off like a ball, like my Da shown me before, when we were doing the fairs. I was little meself them days, no bigger than Madoc.

'So now I make wood balls, one for each of them, then dig out the centre of each one, making a well for the woodshavings. It has to be one for each. I know these two charvers of old. Make sommat for one, the other goes berserk. Then that's trouble for me, I can tell you. All the time I worked there, from when they were little, they would do things like that to torment me. Then stand by and watch with their bright eyes while their Da, or even their Ma, gave me a good hiding.

'I could charm them though, with the stories and fancies that my Da had taught me when I was on the road with him, peddling and playing the fiddle, earning our way from village to village. You should'a heard him sing the song, tell the tale, charver. I tell you those tricks saved me many a beating. One way or other they delayed a wealth of vengeance.

' "Here now!" I say to them. I make two lacy cradles from twine I have in my pocket and lodge each ball in its own cradle. "Now we need to set them alight."

'"What?" shrieks Janey, "You burn'm and we won't have'm. Another gippo trick!"

'Madoc whines on too. No words, just whine...

'"Hold yer whisht, littl'n," says I. "They won't burn proper. Watch!"

'So, I sets the balls on a flat stone, then, getting a spark from my flint, I lights the woodshavings. See? They flame up for a few seconds, then settle down to a smokey kind of glow.

'"Now!"... I pick up both of the quickwood balls by the twine, and hold them out at arm's length, then start to swing them. To and fro at first, quite slowly. Then faster into a big arc— round and round and round. The smoke starts to pour out and the smoke wheel is made. Then the humming starts, loud-soft, loud-soft, like a great whining voice. The ghost of the tree where the wood came from see?

'Well that Janey and Madoc, those charvers, is screaming and laughing at the same time. Dead happy...

'"Me! Me! I want a go!" yells Janey.

'I pull the balls to a stop, then give her one. She starts to whirl it round, getting into a ring straight away, which is pretty good for a littl'n. I have to shorten the twine for Madoc, 'cause he's so short himself. Nearly a dwarf. Even then, when he tries, he can't get away with it at all.

'He throws the thing on the ground and

starts yelling at me. "You broke mine! You broke mine!"

'Well ... he comes across and starts to pummel me, landing hard blows. Now, like I said, I don't like anyone too close to me anyway. So what I do is, I hold him off, then fling him away, so he goes sprawling against the tumbled wall of the Three Spike Barn. He drops like a sack, blood off his head dripping onto an outjutting stone...

'Janey drops her smoke ball and races across screaming, yelling. 'You've killed him, Pip, killed him! Me Da'll kill you. Kill you.' She keeps saying this while I stare at the lad crumpled there beside the wall. Then her voice pierces through, and I am thinking about them up at the house. They mustn't hear this. They mustn't hear this.

'I go to her and clap my hand over her mouth. She bites and kicks and struggles, her body soft and strong at the same time. I get real mad. Suddenly the knife that made the touchwood balls is in me hand. I can feel it plunging into her, in her. No harder than a rabbit or a baby pig. She screams a louder, higher scream, and my hand does it again, with me not willing it, I tell yer. One more time, and she jolts there in my arms and lies still. Then no more noise, no more voice.

'Me hands and me jerkin they're covered with blood. I lean over to drop her to the ground, see, real soft. I watch me own tears splashing onto the blood on my hands, thinning it down like limewash on walls. Then I'm shouting at her, telling her she made me do it, made me do it. I'm there on my hands and knees snuffling and barking out like some animal, just like some animal. As certain as the sun that Reuben'll kill me for this.

'Well, another wisp of hay floats down from the hayloft and settles on Janey's hair and this brings me to, see? I jump up and go down to the river and plunge the top half of me right in, clothes and all. I watch the water soften the hardening blood and swirl it downstream. Soon I am clean enough. Turning round I see Madoc's blood is on the wall, Janey's is on the ground. Just beside them are the touchwood balls, the toys I made them. Smoke is still curling up from the little wells I dug in the touchwood.

'I pick them up, the balls, then I throw them one after another high into the air and into the barn. They make great smoke arcs and have a sparking tail, like stars, some nights. They squeal their high-pitched song, before they plunge into the heart of the dry hay.

'I stand watching as the hay smoulders, then bursts into flowers of light, which crackle and jump across into the sky. The whole thing is alight now, right up to and past where the charvers is lying.

'Well, I turn like, and my foot trips on the knife, still sticky and lying on the ground. I fling that right into the heart of the fire, then it's to the river again to wash the blood off my hands.

'Then I run. I am shivering from the soaking in the river.'

Ian rubbed his hands and blew on them. 'You got away then?' Ian had let the boy go on telling his story, sitting still even when his own flesh had lost its recent heat and turned icy cold.

Pip Wales crouched down in silence inside his halo of leaves, his dark eyes dull, his round face pinched. A wall of even greater chill rolled towards Ian, injecting another level of ice into his frozen body. He waited for the boy to go, to fade from his sight again. But he was still there, solid as an apple.

'Well? Did you get away?' he repeated, shouting into the silence.

'I just walked off, up the valley. When I looked back I could see Three Spike burning high up into the sky. I could hear the cracks and shots as the timber split.'

'Did they come for you?'

'They came after me, like, in no time, really. It was when they brought me down off the moor, when the fire burned down, that the charvers was missed. They thought I'd just fired the barn, see? But then they found the charvers. The charring ... the burned iron of my knife as well.

'Reuben beat me senseless there and then

with his bullwhip, helped on by kicks from the others, like. I tried to tell them about it, to explain, but they wouldn't let me say. Just kept on beating me. I tried to tell them again in the courthouse but they just said I was evil, devil-possessed and called it the babbling of the devil, and said what they had to do. And brought me up here to do it. Then they could have their game. Their own game.'

The boy's voice thinned out. Desperately Ian leapt to his feet, trying to keep the boy with him. 'Why d'you come here, now? Telling us this?'

'I thought you'd know. Down there at the Three Spike leapin' about with those charvers. I thought you'd be the one that'd know.'

'Know what? I don't know what you're saying. I tell you I don't know what you're saying.' Ian was so cold. He jumped down from the stone, stamped his feet hard on the ground and shook his hands and head to get the cold out of them, the feeling back in. He kicked out his legs and turned a full circle.

Relief flooded into him when he turned round a second time. The boy had gone, the only sign of him was the moving, rustling of branches.

Ian leapt away, across the clearing up onto the main road, rubbing his arms and legs as he ran, to take way some of the numb coldness. Lorries and cars flashed past, dazzling his eyes. He put up his thumb for a lift but the cars kept roaring past into the town.

Finally a bus lumbered to a stop and he hopped on. The driver looked at him enquiringly. Pushing his hand in his pocket, he pulled out some of the change from his purchase of the chocolate earlier that day, and spoke his destination.

*   *   *

The woman opened the door a few inches and looked down at him, her eyes floating like fishes behind her thick-lensed glasses. 'Yes?'

'I want to see her.'

'Who?'

'Miss Waterman.'

The narrow mouth pulled to one side. She closed the door till there was only a pencil of light to show it wasn't locked. He could hear voices, one high piercing and angry, the other more familiar, soft and conciliating.

The door opened. Miss Waterman stood there, her dark hair wisping out into a halo in the light that streamed from behind her. He thought of the boy with his halo of leaves.

'What is it, Ian? You shouldn't be here. Really you shouldn't.'

'I come to ask you about sommat.'

'What?'

'You know the boy? The one Jimmy drew from the stone? I seen him again.'

She came round the door and shut it behind

her. She had a bunch of keys in her hand. 'Look. I'll run you home. You can tell me on the way.'

She hustled him towards the van. She gripped his shoulder too hard as she manoeuvred him into the passenger seat. The bubble of story inside him popped and vanished.

She crashed the car into gear, switched on the lights and pulled away. 'Now,' she said, peering through the windscreen. 'What was it?'

'Aw, nothing, Miss.'

'You said you saw the boy.'

'Well I might have.'

'Did you or didn't you?'

'I don't know ... I ...'

The windscreen wipers ground their way through the silence as the rain began to seep down from the sky. Ian started to rub his legs and arms again.

Rachel sighed. 'We'd better get you straight home, Ian. I really can't think what you're up to.'

She watched him trail up the path to his house, and fought down the instinct to run after him, to insist he tell her about the boy he had seen; what fantasies he was driven to now. But there was that mad letter from his mother. Maybe her own mother was, for once, right. It was crazy to get involved. She released the handbreak very gently and drove off just as he was putting his key in the door.

*   *   *

Ian let himself into the empty house, put on the gas fire, and made himself some tea and a bowl of cornflakes. He turned the gas up full and crouched in front of the fire on a low stool.

He was still staring at the flickers with their transparent blue halo, the lick of red at the base, clutching a cold and empty cup, when Maureen Sobell's key turned in the lock. Her glance went absently over him as she came into the room. 'Who told you you could come in the house? Put that fire down a notch, Ian, you'd think we were made of money.'

A spurting rush echoed off the scullery walls as she filled the kettle with water. Then she came back to lean on the frame of the door between the rooms. 'You didn't ask where I'd been.'

'Bingo?'

'No. I've been to the station. Taxi there with the cases. Taxi all the way back just for me. Our Sandra's gone. Rush job. Manchester then London, they said. Clubs. Could be her big chance ... Ian! What the hell ... Stop, will you?'

He was leaping up the stairs two at a time. Sandra's bedroom door was wide open, as was the door of her empty wardrobe, as were her curtains, letting in the grey light of the street. The dressing table was stripped bare. There were dry yellow rings where the glass bottles and jars had stood on the polished wood.

Ian threw himself full length onto Sandra's bed. He had never lain on her bed before. Never.

'Well, now, pet.' Maureen was standing in the doorway, a cigarette in her hand. He had not noticed that her make-up had run, and her eyes were red rimmed. 'You're right, Ian. She'll be a big miss, our Sandra. But that Bayers bloke insisted. He's going, so she's gotta go. No job for her here now. Better chance to be seen down there. Could be her big chance, couldn't it?'

He smoothed the pink bedcover with his hand. She started to go back down the stairs, but turned and popped her head round the bedroom door. 'So there's just you and me, now, isn't there? We'll just have to watch out for each other, won't we?'

'Yeah,' he said. 'Yeah.' He felt his arms and legs carefully with his fingers. They were icy cold again. As cold as they had been there out at the crossroads talking to Pip Wales. He knew he would never be warm. Never again.

CHAPTER EIGHT

A GOOD SUNDAY

Rachel Waterman hated Sundays at home. With their uncomfortable combination of leisure, guilt and generalised suspicion, they had always defeated and confounded her. College Sundays had been wonderful. Voluntary chapel which she had attended, sumptuously High Anglican rich in perfume and the old poetry of the King James Bible; then formal lunch with the girls in their already obsolescent 'afternoon dress' which had been on the required list which accompanied her acceptance to college; then walks through Northumbrian meadows with a few friends who taught her to loosen out, to trust her feelings, to relish and not look down her nose at the art of being silly. Sumptuous Sundays.

At home it was different. When she was small, her mother would say, 'I should go to chapel. I really should. But with the Sunday dinner, the baby and then your father not fit to be left. No trusting him on his own...' There was something about him setting fire to the place once, and leaving the bathroom tap on so the kitchen ceiling fell down.

Her mother never went to chapel. Rachel went there each Sunday as her mother's agent;

a chapel-going surrogate. Chapel was hearty enough in a buttoned-down kind of way, but the only passion was communicated when a handsome, if somewhat earnest, lay preacher, who dug coal for his living during the week, shared with them his visions of hell.

So Rachel would go off every Sunday in her brown velour hat, feeling that she was leaving behind something very special which only became complete, locked into place, when she was absent. As she sang the rollicking hymns she could see, in her mind's eye, her father with his arms round her mother, who had Elena in her arms, all dancing around. She could sense the togetherness of the three of them while she was away. She could see them wrapped in their warm circle as she sang the songs and listened to the stories from the gospels and the Old Testament. She preferred the Gospel stories; those from the Old Testament were a desperate worry for her: walls tumbling down, seas rushing in and words on tablets of stone. The story about Lot's wife made her lose sleep; she started to worry that if she did turn round one Sunday morning, to look at the three of them, or even think about the three of them, she too might turn to a pillar of salt.

Then Elena became old enough for her own velour hat, but was listened to when she cried off going to chapel. At that time the imperative for some person from the family to represent the house by going to chapel seemed to fade. So

Rachel could stay home on Sundays, only to find that Sundays did not involve dancing. They were filled with long stretches of weary time, programmes on the Home Service and the residual smell of boiling cabbage.

For a time she tried going to chapel under her own steam, but the handsome preacher had left and it was not the same.

The only religious aspect left in the house was the custom of Sunday dinner; a deadening ritual made worse by the fact that her mother did not have the artifice to turn it into ritual art.

The best linen, the best china was put out. Flowers bought on Saturday were placed bang in the centre of the table. Her mother served Yorkshire puddings with lumpy onion gravy; then a fresh plate of watery vegetables with beef.

The Yorkshire puddings emerged from the oven in consistencies ranging from leather to unleavened sponge, occasionally descending to concrete. These were put onto the table with a defiant crash, and an unspoken challenge for anyone to comment.

Rachel's father, a quiet man, would never have dreamed of commenting. His Sundays consisted of rummaging in the gardens to little effect. Apart from that he would take the papers up to the caravan and sit in there and read them. Rachel, sent up to call him in for his tea, often found him fast asleep in his threadbare, discarded chair.

Her father was not strong. His working week of trailing around the large estate with his credit book, trying to squeeze club payments out of unwilling customers, was exhausting and sometimes dangerous.

One Saturday, when Rachel was thirteen, one of his customers knocked him violently down some steps instead of paying him. He came home and made little of it. When Rachel went up the garden to wake him for his Saturday tea—fruit scones and egg sandwiches as usual—he was sitting up, struggling to breathe.

He was dead within eight hours, the hospital saying bland things about rib damage and a punctured lung.

These days, Elena made sure Sunday dinners were much more rushed affairs. Today, for instance, she had dashed in from an urgent game of tennis for her Yorkshire puddings and vanished just as quickly. Elena simply did what she chose and took no notice whatsoever of their mother. Their mother protested that Elena did all these things on a 'good Sunday' but as far as Rachel could tell, their mother thought more of Elena for it. Silently she cheered her sister on, but her own habits of submission were too strong. So she still sat through the watery vegetables and the rice pudding before escaping upstairs to her room.

This Sunday afternoon she put the very final touches to the Class Book which recorded and illustrated their walk to the Old Baths, and wrote up her work-forecast for the following week, to be given to Jack Marriot in Mr Warner's absence. Then she went downstairs and read *Bonjour Tristesse* sitting in the window-seat while her mother dozed in the chair.

She went for her usual walk, through the trim streets of what her mother called the select end of the town. On this Sunday she decided, with great finality, that she would leave home. School was bad enough, but she liked the children; they made her laugh and enjoy their silliness, just as she had enjoyed that of the girls in college. Perhaps she would teach in London or Manchester. Perhaps there the schools, the parents, would be different. Perhaps there would be a man, like the fire-eating preacher she had been drawn to at the chapel, that time. Perhaps, there, Sunday would be a real day, not a tired re-run of some old black and white film.

She knew this decision to escape would bring on one of those low-level rows at which her mother was such an expert, with assertions about sacrifice and ingratitude, and whines about looming poverty.

But she would survive that. It would be worth it to get out.

Mrs Waterman was in the kitchen when Rachel returned from her walk. She was spreading best quality margarine on white bread, eggs chopped and ready beside her. The radio was rattling away in the corner.

Rachel watched with revulsion the deliberate way her mother spread the yellow grease to the very corners of the bread.

Her mother caught her eye. 'It says there's been a murder,' she said casually, conversationally. 'Two, in fact.'

Rachel hung up her coat, pulling her sleeves back the right way out. Sundays did tend to be murder days, she thought. The Sunday papers spread around her mother's chair were full of them. The *News of the World; The People*. Her mother devoured them.

Sundays are murder, she said to herself, quite pleased at the neatness of two thoughts placed together.

'Two children,' her mother persisted, frowning at her, impatient at her stubborn lack of reaction. 'In the town.'

'Which town?'

'This one.'

'What?' Rachel put out her hand to stop the plump hand spreading the margarine.

Her mother smiled victoriously and started to spread the chopped egg neatly on the bread. 'On the radio. They said two children had been found dead in Oak Ridge. *Foul Play Is Suspected.*'

Rachel gripped harder on her mother's arm. 'Did they say who? Names ... ages?'

'No names. Five and six, they said.'

114

Rachel breathed a sigh of relief and instantly was swept with guilt. Not one of 'her' children, though. Not one of hers. She sat down hard.

'Leave go of my arm, will you? I'll never get these sandwiches done,' said her mother.

'Did they say who'd done it?'

'No. They're setting up an Incident Room.'

'Where? Where did it happen?'

'They mentioned Siskin. And those dreadful old baths. Filthy old place. I didn't know they were still there. Council should have ... What's the matter? What on earth's the matter with you?'

Rachel had started to shake. Her mother put on the kettle. 'No need to take on, Rachel. These things happen. Every day. Look at the papers.'

At that moment Elena burst through the door, her eyes blazing with life, her very limbs crackling with energy.

Rachel started to cry.

'Hey Rache ... what's up?' Elena came and put thin strong arms around her. 'What's up, you old goose?'

'She's just upset, that's all,' said her mother, sulkily. 'You know what she's like. Cries for the world, sometimes. There was something on the news.'

Elena looked at her mother with cold eyes. 'She's still upset. Everybody can't be as hard as nails like you and me, Ma.' That reference was left in the air for a moment. 'What is it, Rache?

115

Why?'

'Two children ... my school I think,' Rachel mumbled. She could see all her children, drawing, writing, running about in the Old Baths. She could see James Denton, tip of the tongue out of the corner of his mouth as he did his pencil-rubbing. She moaned.

'Well, Ma? Are you going to make her a cup of tea, or get her a glass of that Christmas brandy of yours, or both?' Elena's voice was hard. Much older than her fourteen years.

Their mother did as she was told, not displeased at this bit of drama. Sundays had not been the same since Sid died, she said pouring herself a brandy in addition to Rachel's.

*   *   *

The next morning Rachel got into the van and was shaking so much that she couldn't put it in gear.

Elena was sitting beside her with her schoolbag on her lap. 'Oh. Poor sausage. You're far too jittery to drive this old heap.' She put a hand on Rachel's arm. 'You get the bus Rache. I'll walk ... run to school. Come on, or we'll both be late. I'll get lines; I don't know about you.'

Later, on the bus, Rachel listened to murmurs of the tragedy. The air was warm, buzzing with suppressed excitement, with words about shame and monsters. The late television bulletins had mentioned battering and suffocation; the neutral announcer's voice emitting restrained concern over footage of familiar Siskin areas and a heart-gripping shot of the rusty grandeur of the gates to the Old Baths.

Two women sitting in front of Rachel were turning the pages of a newspaper. 'String'm up, by their you-know-whats. That's what they should do. String'm up.'

'Castration,' said the other, satisfaction creaming up in her voice. 'Castration. Least they should do.'

Rachel wriggled uncomfortably in her seat. He's poisoned you with his own evil, thought Rachel. They always do. Murderers. She swallowed the thought.

The iron gates of the school were tangled up with vans and bodies. Men were walking round with bulky cameras. A short tubby man with a long upper lip spoke to Rachel, looking her directly in the eyes. He smiled with a professional sympathy which made her flesh creep. 'You a teacher here, love?'

'Yes.' She could hear the whirr of a camera.

'What about these kids, the ones who—'

'I don't know who they are.'

He checked a notebook. 'Michael Davis. Jonathan Davis. Aged five and six.'

Her body sagged. 'I don't know them,' she said, pushing hard past him. Of course. Davis.

She *did* know them. Half-brothers to James Denton. Tough little things. They clustered round James outside the school gates, protecting him like a pair of wasps from the hassle which he inevitably got, being a bit slow.

The staff room was packed, their staff augmented by staff from the Infant and Junior Schools which were on the same site. The lack of space was aggravated by the bulk of a wheelchair containing Mr Warner who was sitting slumped to one side, his face grey.

The faces turned to her. Margaret Rawlings looked ten year older than her forty years, her face lumpy and blotchy with tears. Rachel had only seen her a time or two; once at the Autumn Fayre, and once at the joint school sports day. She must be Michael and Jonathan's teacher. She was tall and raw-boned, her large hands always busy fashioning some fantastic artifact for her children, making a bright haven of her classroom. Now those hands were clasped tightly together in awful stillness.

Miss Priestley spoke. 'You heard, Miss Waterman? Those Davis children. Out of control, these children...'

Mr Warner sat up in his chair, noisily clearing his throat. Rachel leaned against a wall.

He waited till she was settled before he spoke. 'I have no doubt, Miss Priestley, that we're all aware of this event. Yesterday, early

118

evening, Mr Marriot was contacted by the police, who naturally came for me. They talked to us at length, right into the night. I was with Mr and Mrs Davis when they identified ... er ... identified. Mr and Mrs Davis ... I taught both of them when they were at this school themselves. It doesn't seem so long ago ...' The fading voice was out of character.

Beside him, looking shrunken and defeated, Jack Marriot stared hard at the floor.

Mr Warner started to speak again. His pedantic phrases dug hard into Rachel's skull; looking into his face she could see desperate concern and a kind of fear. 'I intend to tell you all that we—that is Mr Marriot and I—know. First, though, it is important for us to recognise that these events, shocking as they are, are especially so to us, as teachers of these two boys. We have had their care in our hands. A sacred trust. So, when something like this happens we are bewildered and angry. Inevitably we find ways to blame ourselves.'

There was a rumble of assent around the room. Tears started their course down Margaret Rawlings' face, retracing the dried tracks of tears shed earlier.

Mr Warner continued. 'Now is the time for us to draw together, to show each other great kindness, to show kindness even to ourselves.' His eyes moved from face to face, stopping at Rachel. 'We may come from different traditions of education, have different ways of seeing our sacred task, but in this we are one. Each one of us set out initially with a high heart, which may have to endure knocks in time. Each one of us wishes to guide and influence the young, ultimately for their own good. The loss of any of our children by death creates an irreparable vacuum for all of us. However, the loss of two of our children, in this terribly violent fashion, creates a void of senselessness, which we, for all our expertise or faith, find hard to explain. I would recommend to you the Book of Job where, in time, some comfort may be found.'

The speech had obviously been prepared, its ponderous and pedantic style reflecting his years as a lay preacher. Normally, his resorting to this style brought a smile to Rachel's lips. However, as the phrases rolled out, she could feel herself relaxing, her fists unclenching. Looking around she could see the same thing happening to the others. Jack Marriott sat up straight and started to look around. Margaret Rawlings' tears dried up again. The individual barriers of fear and misery which they had all brought in with them began to crumble.

'Now!' he went on more briskly. 'This is our information from the police: The two boys went out yesterday afternoon. They were missed by five o'clock. The Davises are a caring family.' He glared at Miss Priestley. 'The whole family, and other people from the street, went out to search for them. The boys were found by their brother James. It is amazing that James, who is a bit slow, as we all know, even thought of going there. It is an obscure place.'

Rachel met his gaze. 'James was there on Wednesday. The whole class was there on a project. James did some really good crayon rubbings. He was so pleased with himself...'

'Project?' He looked at her, rubbing his narrow glossy chin, then turned very deliberately to look at Jack Marriot. 'A project?' he repeated. 'Well... it appeared that the older child had been battered with stones, which were heaped on top of him. The younger one had been suffocated. Stones on him too.' Warner drew out a snowy white handkerchief and blew his nose.

The unspoken question hung in the air between them all.

'According to the officers, there was no obvious sign of ... interference of a sexual nature.' He looked again at the man beside him. 'Mr Marriott, I think it must be time for the bell. We can leave those children out there no longer as prey for ... the gentlemen of the press. I'd abjure you all to avoid completely any conversation with any section of the media, or any detailed talk with people outside this school; with strangers. That will help neither the boys' family nor the police. If you wish to talk about all this, talk to each other, or to the police. Talk to me. My door is always open. And you all know my home.'

Jack Marriott leaned over and pressed the button beside the blocked-in fireplace; the bell vibrated through the empty corridors of the school.

On her way out, Rachel touched Margaret Rawlings on the arm. 'If there is anything I can do, Miss Rawlings, any way I can help...'

The gaunt woman's grim nod had some gratitude in it. 'Thank you Miss Waterman. But you'll have your own hands full, I think. James is in your class, isn't he?'

There was absolute chaos in Rachel's classroom when she went in. Her call for silence went unheard; she could not even hear it herself. She moved across to the blackboard and with the thick end of the chalk she wrote QUIET on the board in letters two feet high. Whether it was the large drama of her movements or the animal squeak of the chalk on the board, the noise subsided.

She stood up on the dais and looked round. She noted with some relief that James Denton's seat was empty. Ian Sobell, with his head in the big history book, had not participated in the chaos. She thought with a brief spark of pleasure about the change in Ian. At least she was making some headway there. She looked around at the mass of the other faces, looking eagerly, almost hungrily up at her.

'Now...' she said.

CHAPTER NINE

THE GAME

The pain in Ian's foot seemed to have receded by Monday morning. He had to walk gingerly, even so. His face was sore at the side where Maureen had hit him again when she had tried to get him to admit taking the money for the chocolate. But he hadn't given in and she'd had to stop.

In the schoolyard that Monday morning, there were no games, no jumping with ropes, no kicking of balls, no Hum-Dum-Dum. Pupils were gathered together in groups, buzzing and whispering. The air ripped with squeals and high-pitched giggles from time to time. Some mothers had returned to the long-discarded custom of walking along to the school with their offspring. Protective instinct tangled up with curiosity revealed itself in tight faces and high voices.

The prattling buzz of the mothers' chat found an echo in the buzz of cameras and recorders clicking on and off as a couple of reporters tried to talk to parents and teachers on their way into school.

Ian slipped through this activity at the back of a crowd of pupils as they swirled in. No teacher paced on duty at the door, so with other opportunists he made his way into the school before the bell. In his own classroom he walked past Jimmy Denton's empty seat at its place on the left, in the front of the room.

The classroom, like the the schoolyard, was in a kind of hysterical uproar, a manic concentration of fear and glee. Ian reached into his desk and pulled out the history book.

The yelling sustained itself. Even when Miss Waterman came in, it went on and on. Using the side of his eyes Ian could see the green blur of the side of her dress. He had always liked that dress, with its bright green-leaf colour.

He saw her mouth, with its big teeth, open as she tried to get the class into some kind of order. Then he saw her move to the board and with a shrieking scraping block of chalk draw on the word QUIET! in letters two feet high. By the time she had finished the 'T' the buzz had finally subsided. She looked all round the classroom in the welcome vale of silence. Ian felt her glance lingering on him.

'Now...' she said, unusually sour, 'no need for all that noise. Fold your arms!'

There was a rustle as all arms were folded, all heads pushed back in the unnatural pose. There was a clatter as some elbows rested themselves on wooden desks.

Jane Brown put up a hand, bold, even in that class of silence.

'Yes, Jane?'

'Please Miss Waterman, Jimmy Denton's

124

not in school this morning.'

'I can see that, Jane.'

'Because he's missin'. And his little brothers. My mam said they're dead. Murdered.'

A thrilled mutter rippled its way through the rows of children. Ian held his breath. He wished they could just get on with the day. He willed Miss Waterman to start the lesson.

'The Mad Strangler did it,' pursued Jane confidently.

'That's enough, Jane. We've all heard the horrible news about James and his brothers,' said Miss Waterman in a hard voice. Ian hated that hard sound. 'But, nobody knows what really happened. We're all upset about it, but there's no need for silly talk. We have to think about those two little boys. And James.'

Words bubbled out of Ian's mouth in spite of himself. 'Prob'ly run away.'

'Just think,' said Jane. 'Run away, right out of the killer's hands.'

'Don't talk bloody soft, Jane Brown,' said Ian fiercely. 'You know nowt.'

'Ian's right,' said Miss Waterman, frowning at Jane. 'We know nothing. So that's enough talk.' Her glance wandered back across to Ian, who had ducked his head back inside the history book. 'Ian?'

The silvery eyes looked into hers. 'Yes, Miss?'

'Did your Nana get that prescription for the penicillin?'

'Yeah, Miss.' He dropped his gaze.

'Is your foot any better?'

'Yeah. The red's nearly gone.' His leg was covered, so she wouldn't see.

'Good. What happened to your face? That's a nasty bruise.'

'Fell against the door, Miss.'

A knowing snigger rippled round the class.

'Mmm ... Anyway,' she turned her attention to the whole class. 'Now, everyone, follow Ian's example! Get out something to read, so we can sort out the dinner numbers, and do the register.'

There was a clatter as they all breathed out and relaxed, stretching their arms out of their uncomfortable folds. There was a cheerful crash of clashed desktops and a low murmur of conversation as they tried Miss Waterman out for level. Ignoring the hum, she dug into her pedestal desk for a pen and opened the register.

Ian read his book.

'In the streets the people spat upon the murderer and threw stones and clods of earth which hit his face, cutting it in seven places ...'

It was an hour later when Mr Marriot made his entry into the classroom, handling the door with uncharacteristic care. There were no clashed doors, no lion's bellow today. He was followed by a middle-aged man in a navy anorak which covered a battered grey suit. A young policewoman followed them both in.

Ian watched as they all shook hands with Rachel and muttered away to each other.

Mr Marriot's deep voice belled out above the noise. 'I'll leave you to it, then.'

He left the room. A flutter of talk rippled around as the pupils turned to each other to ask questions. Miss Waterman spoke to them in a loud strained voice that was hardly hers.

'Sit quietly, 2X. Mr Saunders is a policeman and he needs to talk to you.'

The silence was powerful then, vibrating in the old walls, the high windows, in the still tense figures of Ian and the others. Their eyes moved from the man in the anorak to the woman in the uniform. The police were not an unfamiliar sight in the square mile of streets. They were down here quite often, sorting out Saturday night fights, knocking on doors to check out people about violent behaviour or petty thieving. The tradition in which they had all been raised was to stay silent around the police. To say nothing.

The detective cleared his throat. 'Now then, you all know what we're here about; it's no good pussyfooting. Lads from this school've been ... murdered. One lad is missing. One from this class. James Denton.' He glanced around at the pictures and the work, so carefully mounted by Rachel and put up on the walls. 'We have to ask you if you know anything about it, anything at all. Have you seen anyone different around in the area? Anyone hanging round? Has James Denton said anything to you?'

There was a long silence.

Then the policewoman spoke. She had fair hair, a tanned face, no lipsick and crooked teeth. Ian thought of Sandra's nice straight teeth, her bright clear lipstick. 'It could be any little thing. Anything unusual. Think hard.'

Her gaze moved systematically from face to face round the room. The silence was only broken by a rustle as Ian Sobell turned a page of his book. Miss Waterman glared at him, then swept her eye over the rest of the class. 'Come on, 2X. There must be something. Any small thing.'

Rachel willed someone to speak, resenting their stolid silence, resenting the urgent presence of the two police officers. Her head felt twice its size and was aching to its very skin.

Mamie broke the silence: 'Jimmy didn't half like doing those rubbing things, at the Old Baths, Miss.' She turned her beady gaze on the policeman. 'He wasn't right, Jimmy, you know. Ten pence to the shilling, my mam says.' Miss Waterman frowned at her, but the detective picked her up very quickly. 'Old Baths? How come he was there? Doing what?'

'We was all there. Our teacher was there.'

Saunder's glance flickered across to Miss Waterman.

128

'It was an Environmental Studies project ...' she began, her cheeks stained bright red.

Jane Brown said, 'We made a book, didn't we, Miss?'

Saunders raised a sparse eyebrow. 'A book?'

'Yes,' said Miss Waterman. 'We went down there, and some other places, and took photographs, did drawings, took imprints. You know the kind of thing ... Then we made a scrap-book ...'

The policeman stayed silent, looking at Miss Waterman with a bland professional neutrality. She went over and pulled the big folder from its plastic bag and laid it on her desk. The police officers stood side by side in silence, turning the pages.

Then Saunders looked up at her, his eyes for the first time less than dead. 'Can we take this?'

'Of course.'

Saunders looked round at them all again. 'Has anybody—anybody—been down the Old Baths since the—er—Environmental Studies thing?'

More silence. Ian closed his history book with great care, leaving his forefinger between the leaves to mark his place.

'... Can you tell me if Jimmy Denton went down there? Did he say anything? About going down there again ...? Has anybody seen anyone—anyone new ... any stranger on the streets, in the district? Round here?'

Silence.

129

Saunders glanced across at his colleague. The policewoman took a step forward, looking urgently round the class. 'You look like a sensible enough lot to me, so maybe I don't need to say this. Get yourselves straight home after school. Stay around your own house. Don't talk to any strangers. If you see anything or remember anything, tell us, or tell your teacher here. You can find us at the community room at the end of Syke Street.

'There'll be one of us there all the time. All day, all night. Anything, anything—come and tell us.' She smiled a wide smile showing her crooked teeth, although her blue eyes were as neutral as those of Mr Saunders. 'Come and tell us,' she repeated.

Then the police officers turned to talk to Miss Waterman. Ian opened his book. The class, released from the spell, started to buzz again, as the policeman muttered away to their teacher, then finally took their leave.

The murmur level from the children rose to a strident rattle, then it faded. They watched as their teacher slumped down onto her tall chair, leaned her elbows onto the table, and covered her face with her hands. She pressed her knuckles into her eyelids. She was seeing in a single flash all the scenes from their walk on Wednesday. The children poring over stones and plants in the baths. Her own self walking down through the fields with the orderly crocodile beside her. James Denton kneeling

130

beside the stone in the silent clearing, rubbing, rubbing.

The noise around her had subsided. She lifted her head, seeing multicoloured stars after the recent pressure on her eyes. The children were silent now, looking at her. Jane Brown looked worried, her eyes were filled with unshed tears. Several faces showed fear, some lips were trembling.

'You all right, Miss?' called Ian Sobell.

'Yes. Just tired. All these things happening.' Making an enormous effort, she smiled round at them. 'Now, let's get on with our day, shall we?'

The rest of the morning proceeded on automatic pilot. The dinner numbers, the register, reading books out, then maths workbooks out, then drawing in jotters when the work was done.

Rachel walked around noticing but not commenting on the drawings which involved Dracula-type monsters and hanged men. Ian Sobell drew what at first looked like a bird in a cage. When she looked closer, she realised it was a man inside the cage. Normally she would have asked questions about it. Today she felt just too tired to bother.

As they finished their drawing she told them to get out a book to read or to look at. Some of them opened books and started furtive conversations, trying not to disturb her as she sat at her desk and leafed blankly through some of their exercise books, her face pale and stiff.

Ian was very tired. There had been a lot to do last night, getting things sorted; then his Nana to face when he got back. Going on about the money and him being a thief.

He put his arm across the history book, his face down on his arm, and slept. He dreamt he was riding down a road on a great horse. Suddenly there was someone on the horse behind him, clinging on so hard that he himself was almost pulled off. The horse galloped on, jumping higher and higher fences. He clasped harder, harder to the reins, then leaned down to grab the mane of the horse, sobbing with frustration at the dragging weight behind him.

He was awoken by the clashing of the school door as Mr Marriot whirled in, saying, without modifying his tone, 'Well, Miss Waterman, that police chappie wants you down there, at the Baths. Something they want to check out with you.'

Marriot turned his massive face to the class. He said, 'Only ten minutes to dinner, you lot. I hope I can trust you to behave. Mmm?'

Then the pair of them were gone in a flurry of bags and coats and short barks from Mr Marriot.

Jane Brown leaned sideways in her seat to look at Ian, a sly grin on her face. 'What're you cryin' for, Ian Sobell? Been nickin' again? Layin' fires? Scared of the police?'

132

He stood up from his chair and left them all behind him, limping out of the room, across the hall and out of the school. He stood in the shadow of a wall and watched an ambulance engorge Mr Warner, immaculate as ever, sitting to attention in a wheelchair.

Rachel Waterman sat still as a mouse beside Mr Saunders as he drove through the streets, then pulled in behind the second of two police cars parked at the Old Baths. A uniformed policeman stood watchfully at the high iron gates which were now half-open. She remembered how she and the children had squeezed through the gap last time. A long time ago.

The detective led her through the gates. She looked down the length of the Baths. There were two policemen poking about in the space, the depression, that had been the bath-void itself.

She jumped as Saunders put his hand on her arm. She looked at it. The nails were scrubbed clean, but too short. Perhaps he bit them, she thought.

'Just stop here, if you will, Miss Waterman. Look. What do you see?'

She looked.

'The Baths. Two of your colleagues searching.'

He called across to the men to come up out of the void telling them to mind where they put their feet. They made their way gingerly upwards, and towards the gate, until they were out of Rachel's eyeline. 'Now,' said Saunders. 'Look.'

She frowned and looked hard, right round the space, wondering what on earth he was on about.

When she did see it, it fell into place like a well designed jig-saw. Consistently, at regular intervals across the space, in too regular a shape to be random, stones had been heaped into quite neat piles like stone cairns. At the bottom of one of the piles was a scrap of something in bright pale blue.

'The piles...' she said.

'Yes?' he said quite urgently.

'They weren't there. There were some piles, but not that many. They weren't that regular.'

'Right. I thought that,' he said, pleased. 'From your photographs, in that scrap-book of yours, several of them are taken from this angle. The piles aren't there in the photographs. Now then, Miss Waterman. Look at it again. What does it look like to you?'

She looked hard. 'They look like cairns, stone cairns... No... it looks like a game,' she whispered slowly. She could see the jumping from place to place. She could hear the shouts, the squeals of glee. 'A child's game.'

She closed her eyes and then opened them to look into Saunders troubled face. 'Are you telling me,' she said slowly, 'That you think a child did this disgusting thing?'

CHAPTER TEN

BLIGHT

Ian and Maureen sat on opposite sides of the kitchen table, eating Maureen's egg and chips, excellent as always. Ian speared three chips onto his fork and munched away, his eyes focussing on the blue flower design on the rim of his white plate. Then he looked up at his Nana. She was wearing a red fluffy jumper. A cast-off of Sandra's; a little short in the arm. The brown make-up was ground into her skin to the shade of old tea.

Ian started to think about one Sunday morning just before Christmas, when the three of them, him, Sandra and his Nana, had sat around this table together.

Sandra had cried off work as she had had a cold. But he thought she looked perfectly fine. Her face was scrubbed clean of make-up and her skin was perfectly white except for a natural pink blush over the cheekbones. Her blonde hair was pulled back in a ponytail, leaving her a fuzzy halo of whispy curls. Ian wished she'd always stay like that and not paint those lines on her eyes; lines that meant she was going out to Mr Bayers, to work. He munched away thoughtfully at his chips, saying nothing. Then and now.

A heavy hand clattered away at the front door. Maureen jumped up guiltily.

Scrutinising her face in the mirror as she passed it, she went out of the room. Ian could hear the babble of talk at the door; her light voice, followed by the heavy tones of a man. She came back, followed by two men, one of them in police uniform.

Maureen stood beside them, smoothing her suddenly sweaty hands down her skirt, looking down at him. 'What have you been doing now, Ian?'

Ian shook his head, spearing another chip and biting into it, hard. He recognised the square face and figure of the man in plain clothes, the man who had been in school that morning.

The policeman checked his notebook. 'It's not like that ... Mrs Sobell is it? We're just checking through the families of all the children at the school, for a start, like. This must be Ian, then? Did we meet this morning, son?'

Ian nodded, his mouth bunged up with chips.

'Well, we're talking to all the people in Ian's class first because, seemingly, they were down the Old Baths last week for, er ...' He checked his notebook again, '... Environmental Studies ... These kids who was killed, their brother was down there for that lesson, seemingly.'

He sat down without being asked, and pulled a pencil out of a deep inside pocket. The uniformed man stood by the door, swaying backwards and forwards, finally coming to rest, leaning right back on the wooden framework.

Maureen sat down in her chair at the table. Her food stayed untouched. Ian munched on, his plate half-empty now.

In a voice weary with routine, Saunders asked Maureen about their whereabouts on Sunday morning. That was easy. She had slept till noon. They always did on a Sunday. No, it was eleven-thirty. Ian brought her tea and toast up then. And the papers. He always did, on a Sunday. '... Then out on some errands, seeing Madge Armitage. Friend of mine.'

Saunders turned his face to Ian, who put down his fork. 'Now, son, how about you?'

'Well, I got up, like.'

'What time?'

'Mebbe nine o'clock.'

'Then what?'

'I listened to the wireless.'

'Then?'

'I read me comics.'

'He's keen on his comics,' interposed Maureen, giving him some kind of support. 'Keeps them for months. Reads the print off the pages.'

'Then...?'

'I made me Nana her breakfast. Used to do it

137

for Sandra too. Toast and tea.'

'Sandra?'

'His Mam. My daughter,' said Maureen flatly.

The policeman looked from one to the other of them with greater interest. The man by the door blew out breath in a way which was nearly a whistle. He was silenced by a swift turn of the head from Saunders. 'Sandra Sobell? We know her. On the … she works for Eddie Bayers.'

Maureen nodded. 'Yes, she works for a living. Not like some lazy oiks around here.'

Saunders turned to the boy. 'Well, son. What about this baths place?'

'We went there with our teacher. It was interesting, like.'

'What'd you do there?'

'Well, some people took photos with the instant camera. Some people drew, some people collected bits and pieces and put them in these plastic bags, some people wrote down words for what they saw…'

'What about the Denton lad? He can't write, can he? His ma said that. Can't read or write. Can't talk, as of Sunday, seemingly. Never said a word after he showed where Michael and Jonathan had played. Then he vanished. So he's not saying anything to anybody.'

'He did rubbings.'

'What are they, when they're out? Rubbings?'

'Paper and pencil. Or crayons. You get

138

texture off stone and things. Jimmy liked it. Really liked it. He did a real good one up at the Old Cross. It really looked like the face of that lad.'

'Which lad?'

'Well, he was there up at the Old Cross. And after.'

'In your class?'

'Nah. Not at our school.'

'Older?'

'Well, he said he was, but he didn't look any older.' Ian looked unblinkingly into the eyes of the policeman. 'He was kind of hanging around.'

The policeman gave a grunt of satisfaction, then sat with his pencil poised. 'Now son, tell me exactly what he looked like.'

'Well, only a bit bigger than me, but heavy. Like them boxers. Big arms. He had this waistcoat thing on ... he had nothing on his feet. Really dirty feet.'

'His face?'

'Just like the face on the rubbing. That rubbing that Jimmy Denton did. It's in the book. The book the teacher gave you.' Ian crossed his knife and fork on the empty plate.

The policeman closed his notebook and stood up. 'That'll do for now, son. Something to go on at least. Likely we'll be back. Mebbe you'll have a bit more for us then.'

Saunders looked down at Maureen, her meal clay-cold in front of her. Not bad looking really. The daughter was a dazzler. Not that that would last long the life she was leading. Her mother was not bad at all for her age. She looked familiar, somehow. Where had he seen her before? 'You'll be around tomorrow if I need you, Mrs Sobell?'

'I'll be out and about,' said Maureen. 'And it's Miss Sobell if you don't mind.'

His thin brow hit his hairline. 'And is she your daughter? The lad's mother?'

Maureen nodded.

'And where might she be?'

'Down in London. She sings with the band.'

The man leaning on the door smothered a laugh.

'Does she now?' said Saunders.

Ian finally broke the ensuing silence by asking Maureen if she had finished with her tea. If so could he have what was left? She pushed her plate to him, and he started on the cold chips.

Saunders was at the door looking back at them. Behind him the face of the man in uniform faded to total shadow in the gloomy hallway. 'I reckon we'll probably be back.'

Maureen eyed them sourly. 'You should be out there getting hold of the feller who murdered those two bairns, instead of hanging round decent people.'

'Well, Mrs S. You never know what's gonna help; even some little thing you might say. Or young feller-me-lad here...'

The front door slammed. Maureen stood up, pulling down her red jumper, smoothing it over her hips, and went to make herself another cup of tea. She stared thoughtfully at the water as it ran with a hard clatter into the kettle.

Oh yes, she'd recognised the marble-eyed policeman. Much older now, and thinner up top. But those eyes and that hunched stance were still the same. Even as a young copper he had prowled around like some underfed wolf. He'd been the one to arrest her the one time she had been caught soliciting. Years ago now. Sandra had been toddling then. Quite small.

She took her cup of tea and walked past Ian as though he wasn't there. He heard her footsteps on the stairs.

Ian was just finishing off the cold food she'd left on her plate when she came back into the kitchen. She had a white fluffy coat over her arm, and was wearing a black dress and black high heels. She had drawn black lines round her eyes and painted her lips with red gloss the colour of fresh blood. Ian thought about Sandra with lipstick on. Her mouth was full, like a strawberry. He thought again that there was nobody, not on the pictures, not in the magazines or the comics, that was as pretty as Sandra. No one could touch her.

He followed Maureen to the door. She looked down at him. 'I'm just out for a chat with Mrs Armitage. You'd better stop in

141

tonight, love. No saying, with this maniac around. Now, no fires or floods, mind. Behave yourself. I want a home to go to. Just lock the door and read your comics. That's all. Nothing else!' She gripped his shoulder too tight.

He nodded and twisted away from her. 'All right, Nana, all right. Don't go on, will you?'

*   *   *

The minute she heard Rachel's key on the lock, her mother moved into the hall from the kitchen. Tall like Rachel, if rather more heavily built, she filled the doorway into the kitchen. She was wearing the dark-patterned long-sleeved frock she always changed into after she had finished her work at twelve o'clock. Over it she wore a neat apron, decorated with the embroidery which was the only domestic skill at which she excelled. 'Well?'

'Well, what?'

'What happened? Did they say?'

The hall was drenched with the smell of Lavendo Polish. Rachel was suddenly conscious of the other smell all about herself; the smell of school, the smell of all those children. 'I've got to go and change,' she said.

She leapt upstairs two at a time straight into the bathroom. The bath was deep, standing on its own clawed feet; the water gushed busily out of the taps. In two minutes her clothes were in a heap on the floor and she was immersed in the

142

water. She shampooed her hair and then poured the shampoo down her body, rubbing and rubbing it into her skin. She only stopped when she was stinging with the pungent smell of pine and herbs, and her skin was very pink and sore.

Once out of the bath, she bundled her school clothes—everything, right down to her bra—tightly in a towel, ready to take downstairs. Then she put on a clean ironed bra, clean Marks and Spencer interlock pants, brown lightweight trousers and a fawn sweater.

'Rachel?'

She made her way down, clutching the towelled parcel to her side. 'Yes?' A surge of familiar dread flowed through her as she noted the two cups of tea poured out at the kitchen table.

'Any more about the children?' Her mother leaned forward, hands clasped tight round one of the cups. 'What else did they tell you? It's been on the wireless all day.'

'Well,' she said dully, pushing the clothes into the washer and heaping in the powder, 'they were brothers of a boy in my class. James Denton.' She realised now how closely she had been linking James with his brothers throughout the day. He was not in his seat in her classroom. He might just as well be dead too.

'Have they got anybody for it?'

'No. Just floundering round, I think.'

143

'Poor things. Poor little things. Was there ... er ... assault? They didn't say on the radio.'

Rachel twisted her lip to one side. 'No. They said not. Just beaten and strangled ... Oh God, what am I saying?'

She pushed the cup forward and, crossing her hands at the wrists, she put her head down on the knuckles and pressed hard on her eyes. Her mother's face, with its mixture of anxiety and eagerness, was blotted out. The stars before her eyes faded and she could see the Baths again, with the heaps of stones, the flush of May weeds and plants. This time she could see the bodies, just where the markers had placed them. And beside them, larger and more bulky, lay the body of James, their brother. His eyes were open and he was looking to the sky, a vague smile on his thickened lips. Tears started coursing through the hills and valleys of her knuckles and fingers.

A hand pressed into her shoulder and she twisted away from it, thinking it was her mother. 'Come on, Rache!' It was Elena's voice. Through the tears Rachel could see her, still in her battered navy school blazer and skirt. 'You can't do anything about it now. You couldn't have done anything. It's outside of you, it's nothing to do with you.'

'It's not outside me! I took them there, to that place.' Rachel jumped up and ran upstairs. She lay down on the bed with her face to the ceiling trying to blank out her mind, to

144

stop the vision of the Baths and the small pitiful bodies of Michael and Jonathan, and their big brother James.

*   *   *

Ian ran down the back streets, enjoying his new freedom of movement. His foot hardly hurt at all now. The doctor's stuff must really be working. Every now and then he changed the parcel to the other hand to give his shoulder a rest. Jogging along, he blessed his luck that Maureen had left the house so distracted, thinking of other things. It was easy, then, to get away from the empty house.

His steps slowed halfway up the long road out of town, and he looked back over the streets and houses. At least one light shone from each house and there were hundreds and hundreds of lights, the streets snaking down in black pathways between them. He thought there must be a family for every light and how many families that must make. He could see the tall cornflake box shape of the building, only dimly lit as far as halfway up. As he watched, he clutched the heavy carrier to him and it was as though he had flicked a switch: the street-lights came on, flaring to a fiery crimson orange before they settled to their hard white glow. It was something, being able to do that.

In ten minutes he had reached the mud-packed clearing. He walked around the space, cocking his ear again and listening to the characteristic deadly silence. No voice this time. No Pip Wales either, although in the dusk he could see the low roof of the farm with its smoke curling up into the night sky. Then straining his ear harder he began to hear the yells and shouts from the farm in the hollow. They were distant, as though he was hearing them through a long tube.

He settled down to his task. The tattered comics made a good pile as he pulled them from his carrier and crumpled them up in front of the stone. Jimmy had knelt here, hadn't he? On that day, kneeling down and making his rubbing from this stone when everyone was standing scared at the eerie silence.

Ian pulled matches from his pocket and carefully lit the comics in five or six places. A pity about the comics. But he had had them a long time, read them a thousand times. Their time was finished.

When there was a good blaze he placed the items from the carrier on the fire, taking care not to block the flames. Each one took fire very easily; added together they made a good blaze. He watched the bright cheerful flames with a pleasure he could almost taste.

Suddenly he started to cough, as his nose and mouth filled with an acrid smell; worse than the smell of the old pool down by the gasworks; worse than the smell in the boys' toilets across the yard at school; worse than the smell outside the abattoir of Charlie Spedder, the popular butcher who killed all his own beasts down at the east end of the town.

Ian felt the piles of cold chips, so assiduously eaten earlier that evening, rise in his crop and into the back of his mouth. He put his hand over his nose and lips ... He heard shouts, a great wailing of voices behind him, and set away to run across the field and onto the road, his hand still pressed hard against his mouth.

After a few minutes' hard running, he turned round. He could see the black smoke of his fire curling up and losing itself in the night sky, smoky black into luminous purple. He turned and trudged the rest of the way home at walking pace, the smell fading from his nostrils, the food subsiding back to his stomach.

The house was empty when he got back. His Nana must still be out having her 'bit of a chat' with Mrs Armitage. Ian stood on the inside of the door to the kitchen, leaning on it, right up against the glass panes, just like the uniformed policeman. Tears came into his eyes, fell unchecked to his chin and dripped onto his shirt, the plaid one his Nana had got him from the jumble sale that was only a bit too big.

It was minutes before he could manage to shake his head and force the tears back. He did not cry. He never cried. He told himself again that he never cried. His head obeyed him. The tears dried up and he leaned over to turn on the wireless.

CHAPTER ELEVEN

THE VISITOR

Walking through the streets back from the house of her friend Moira Armitage, Maureen Sobell felt uncharacteristically disturbed. The cultivated calmness which had helped her keep going for years seemed to be draining away from her; that numbness which meant that she could sidestep the aggression and bad feeling which had flooded in her direction for twenty-odd years, since she had returned to Siskin.

Sometimes she would lash out, just to get rid of the numbness, just to break the skin of things; to feel more alive. Not that she ever lashed out at Sandra. When she was with Sandra the worst of the feeling went. At least with Sandra she felt fractionally more alive. It was Ian who got the worst of it; she was aware of that. Usually Ian got the wrong side of her tongue, or the wrong side of her fist. But he could be so irritating, so sly; so like the stupid lad who'd fathered him and ruined Sandra's prospects. Someone had to show him the way; make him toe the line.

But today the tone of voice and the knowing

looks of that copper Saunders had really unsettled Maureen. He reminded her of a time in her life she had closed off; chosen to forget.

The problems were not her fault. Anyone could see that. It had started with Sandra, a baby, seductively beautiful from the first day, and herself still a teenager. She had no work, no money; her parents had first branded her a slag and then turned her out. Her father's attitude changed from one of fondling and confident suggestiveness to a vengeful and jealous accusation. Her mother, always a rival, was only too pleased, finally, to get her out of the house.

Just before and just after Sandra had been born, Maureen lived in a big stone house by a river, with other girls who had to face having their baby on their own. They were cared for with stunning neutrality by a team of brisk women who insisted the girls learn basic skills of scrubbing floors and wiping down surfaces, washing nappies and making up feeds.

She'd moved on from there with two of the girls from the stone house, Sheila and May. Sheila had somehow got hold of a flat up in the town. Business girls, she'd said; they would be business girls. She knew the score did Sheila. She'd been in business before.

Sheila got them organised. One of them would watch the babies while the other two worked the streets and the pubs. They went into cars and up back alleys to earn their money, the income coming from the quantity rather than the quality of the encounters.

Maureen loathed the work, but the men never came to the flat, and she liked life with the girls. Like Sheila and May, she despised the men but took their money.

She found though, that she was never happy. When it was her turn to mind the three babies, the crying and the routines of feeding and changing made her very bad tempered. For her it was worse than the work in the pubs and the back alleys. However, May loved being with the children, so Maureen found herself offering to do her street turns as well, so long as she kept Sandra happy.

The comradely life in the flat lasted for four years. It only finally broke up when Maureen and May were arrested for soliciting. At first Maureen was quite philosophical about it; this was their first time, after all. Then she had the life frightened out of her by a visit from a zealous young social worker who threatened to remove Sandra into care.

That was it. With one look at Sandra, all pink and white with golden sausage curls tied in a blue ribbon, Maureen was away from the town and the flat. She came back to Oak Ridge, to the blighted streets of Siskin where she had grown up. She worked quite hard in a local factory to make some kind of a life for Sandra and herself, occasionally, discreetly, doing a bit of the old business when funds were very low.

There was perverse satisfaction when Sandra in her turn, with a nice irony, became pregnant. Unlike her own parents, Maureen was there for Sandra. She had been a good mother to Sandra, hadn't she? They would be a team. She would mind the baby while Sandra went on making her way, and her money, with her singing and her better life.

The drawback was that Maureen was no better at the baby thing with Ian than she had been when Sandra was a baby, and this time there was no motherly May hovering around, mothering the world.

So Ian, the boy-baby, had to make do with her. Well, she thought she hadn't coped bad, considering what a little devil he was. She mostly stayed calm, even if sometimes he did get under her skin.

But that copper, today, with that flicker of recognition, had broken her calm. The rush and the hate. The waste and the sinister abuse of those working years flooded back to her. He had come back to remind her of all that stuff she had salted away.

And who was it who had made him come? Had brought all that filth flooding back into her aching head?

It was that teacher. That bloody teacher. The more she thought about it, the more she thought it was all about the teacher. The teacher had fussed on about Ian's foot, as though it were really something. She had got the doctor round to make trouble. Then the fussy cow had put Ian into those fancy girl's clothes...

Now the police would keep on the watch for Sandra, Maureen just knew it; her career and her singing ruined before she could even start to make her way to the big time.

Then there were those kids. Those poor little sods who got themselves killed. It was because of that teacher that those kids were there, at the Baths at all. She'd had them down that filthy place, with her fancy play-teaching. She'd opened the way for all this. Those kids there, in those old Baths, planted for some pervert to come along and kill them. That bloody teacher!

When Maureen walked into the house Ian was sitting curled up into the smallest easy chair staring at the television screen which had some images of men and tanks, then the face of the newscaster. There was no sound. He had the volume turned right down.

'What you sitting there like some gormless idiot for?' She stared absently at the moving images herself, for a minute. 'Where'd you say that teacher lived, Ian? Where'd she take you home?'

Ian yawned, gulping for breath. 'That big long street coming down from the ridge. The houses have big windows. You get the Number Three bus.'

'What number? The house, what number?'

He looked at her, frowning. Something was up, he could tell. There was an excitement about her, a buzz. Sometimes, when she got a bee in her bonnet she would mizzle on about it until he just wanted to scream and hit out at her. One day he would take her on. But not today. He was too tired now to play any of his games, or any of hers, for that matter.

'Ninety-nine,' he yawned. 'I remember that. Two nines.'

'Good.' She re-tied the scarf round her neck and pulled on her gloves. 'Right. You get yourself to bed, son. Look at those black rings round your eyes. You need your sleep. We all do, all these folks coming to disturb us. They need telling.' She brought a neatly folded half-bar of chocolate out of her pocket. 'Here y'are. Had it left from earlier.'

He pushed it back at her, staring hard at it. 'Don't want it.' he said.

She was very angry for a split second, and he braced himself. Then she laughed and threw the chocolate onto the table.

'Well, mebbe you'll get peckish after. Anyway. Remember. Straight to bed, I'll lock the door behind me.'

The door slammed behind her. Ian sat down at the table, opened Maureen's paper and cast his eye over the main picture, which was of the funeral of the American President. His wife was there, nearly as pretty as Sandra. And

153

children too, in coats with rows of black buttons. He put a finger on their pale faces.

* * *

'Manchester?' Mrs Waterman's voice rose to an incredulous squeak. 'What on earth is there for you in Manchester?'

'Schools. New purpose-built comprehensives with wide windows and dining rooms,' said Rachel stubbornly. She was leaning against the door jamb in her dressing gown.

'Dirty place, Manchester.'

'So is Siskin.'

'But this is Oak Ridge. Siskin's just a blighted place on the edge. They're pulling it down next year. It's in the paper. It's lovely up here on the Ridge. Nothing like it in Manchester.'

'I bet there is.'

Her mother folded her arms across her neat apron. 'It's this business, isn't it? The business with the children? Driving you away!'

Elena looked up from her magazine. 'Leave it, Mother,' she said warningly.

'It's not to do with the children. Not at all. I was thinking this before. Some girls from college are working in Manchester. They have a flat.'

'You want nothing with flats. I know what goes on in flats. It's all over the *News of the*

154

World.'

'You read the wrong papers, Ma,' said Elena.

Her mother shot her a murderous glance. She turned to Rachel. 'Well, if it is about the children, Rachel, just think how many more maniacs there'll be in Manchester compared with a little place like this. Like I say, you want nothing there. Dark Satanic Mills, and all that.'

Rachel looked at her steadily and took a breath. 'It's not a maniac, Ma. Well, not ... The police think—the detective is saying—'

She was interrupted by a thunderous knocking on the door. Rachel raced upstairs, stood by her bedroom door and ran her fingers through her hair, still coiling down in snakes after her bath. She put her hand on the doorknob then hesitated as she heard raised voices, shouting coming from the hall. She turned and made her way to the first turn of the bannister.

Looking down to the well-lit hall, she saw the backs of Elena and her mother. Beyond them she looked into the face of Maureen Sobell, brown with make-up, with its black lined eyes...

Maureen looked upwards and saw Rachel. 'Here she is, then. You, Miss bloody teacher! I need to talk to you.'

Rachel was puzzled. What was Ian's grandmother doing here? Her mind was full of

James Denton and his brothers. She set off down the second flight. 'What is it, Mrs Sobell?'

'I've told her she can't talk to you,' said Elena. 'Don't talk to her, Rache. She's got some bee in her bonnet. You're in a bad enough state already...'

Rachel's mother said nothing, but stood glaring from one to the other of them, her arms crossed at her waist clutching herself tightly.

Rachel was on a level with them now. 'What is it you want, Mrs Sobell?'

'I've come to tell you, you nosy bitch, you interfering little cow, to keep your neb out of people's lives. Look what it's come to now. Our Ian not knowing if he's on his arse or his elbow, ashamed of what he stands up in, and more and more sly by the day. And two bairns dead as doornails in a place you opened up. And one run away to God knows where. You bloody stuck up cow! Playing around with those kids instead of teaching them proper.'

'I'm sorry, Mrs Sobell...' began Rachel.

'You, with your bloody mournful looks. "I'm sorry Mrs Sobell, sorry Mrs Sobell..."' yelled Maureen in a cruelly perfect imitation of Rachel's genteel tones. Then she leapt across and grabbed Rachel's hair with one hand, lashing out and punching away at her face and shoulder with the other. She clung to the larger girl like a limpet, balancing herself to land the rain of blows.

156

Mrs Waterman screamed, and kept on screaming. Elena tried without success to pull the woman away from her sister. Then she vanished into the kitchen and came back with a bucket of water, which she emptied over the pair of them.

Maureen gasped and let go of Rachel, and Elena grasped her by the shoulders and pushed her along the hall and out of the front door, locking and bolting it against her. From the outside, Maureen Sobell started to batter the door and yell words which they couldn't hear.

Rachel sat down quickly on the stairs, her head and shoulders dripping with her share of the rescuing water. Mrs Waterman had stopped her screaming and was reaching for the telephone.

'What're you doing?' said Rachel wearily.

'Getting the police. That was assault. The woman should be in jail...'

'Don't do that, mother. The police have plenty to do without this. Anyway it'll just prove her right.'

'How do you make that out?' said Elena, dabbing away at her sister with a towel. 'She's right. The woman wants locking up.'

'Anything to do with me, and there's trouble. You heard her.'

'Don't talk rubbish,' said Mrs Waterman, her hand lingering on the receiver.

Elena took the telephone firmly away from her mother. 'There's no way she should have the police, if she doesn't want them. Leave it, Ma.'

Her mother blew hard down her nostrils and pushed past them both into the kitchen, slamming the door behind her.

Elena sat down beside Rachel on the fawn carpet. 'Hard for you, Rache, isn't it? All this? You want everybody to be happy; all your kids to be angels; all their parents to know how good you are. So what do you get? A good hiding! And a bald patch where she's pulled your hair out by the roots.' She picked a strand of hair from Rachel's shoulders. 'It's not nice, but maybe you'll have to harden up. You know. Get a thicker skin.'

'It's more than that Elena. Those dead children...'

'Yeah. I see that. But when they catch the bloke that did it maybe things'll settle down a bit.'

Rachel turned her sister to face her and looked her full in the eyes. She could feel a bruise clotting about her upper cheek-bone. 'But that's the point, Ellie. I was there. Detective Saunders had me back at the Baths. I was trying to tell you. It wasn't a bloke. Or it might not have been...'

'Cripes! You can't really think ... he doesn't think a child did it ...!'

'No ... Children ... maybe. That whole space was set up for a game. You could see it. There were children there...'

158

*　　*　　*

Next morning, the fine May weather broke down into a drizzling cold, and Rachel put a cardigan on top of her leaf-green dress. Elena wanted her to stay at home, but she refused. She pinned up her hair to cover the bald patch and put green, then flesh-coloured make-up on the bruise. She thought absently of leaving the green patch as it was. It would tone with the dress and, at least, give the children a chuckle. She was one of them now, bruises on her face.

She was just pulling on her mackintosh in the hall when the doorbell rang. She opened the door to Detective Saunders. He had a very solid look about him, with his square face and his clean white shirt.

'Mr Saunders. You've found someone...'

'No, Miss Waterman. Wish we had. I'm here to ask you a favour.'

She showed him through to the sitting room and sat him on the fawn moquette sofa with its green embroidered cushions. She clicked on the electric fire to take the chill off the room and sat opposite him, her legs slightly apart, her hands dropped between her knees in the loose folds of her coat.

Elena put her head round the door, put her thumb up, then vanished. Rachel knew she would keep their mother away. 'What can I do? What can I do for you?'

He wriggled a little under her earnest gaze.

159

'It's James Denton, Miss Waterman. He's turned up in a barn half way up the valley.'

'Is he hurt?'

He shook his head. 'A bit mucky and dusty, but apart from that ... He's at home now. His mother's relieved to see him, but she's walking around in a daze, poor lass, bunged full of tranquillizers. His dad's trying to cope with the family, not quite realising what's happening around him. And young James is sitting in a corner saying nowt. Not to them; not to us. And we need him to talk to us. He's gotta know something.'

'You think he's...'

'Nah ... Dunno. Might have heard something, seen something. I'm still not sure ... Looks harmless enough himself. But then, people do, until you know about them and suddenly you can see the harm. It's not a change in them, mind. It's a change in the way you see them; the way you look at them.'

'Well, I do know James. He couldn't be involved. I'm certain he'd never have done this. He's a big lad, but he's like a little mouse inside.'

'Well, if you could talk to him, get him to talk to you. There might be something, some small thing that could help.'

She would have to do it. She sighed. 'Yes. All right ... When?'

'Now. We can't lose any time.'

'I'll have to telephone school.'

'No need. I rang Jack Marriott. No need to look surprised. Old friend of mine, Jack. Same cricket club. He's the treasurer and I'm twelfth man. He's been a good cricketer in his time, has Jack … Anyway, he'll do the necessary at the school. Don't you worry.'

She stood up and straightened her coat, buckling the belt. He stood up close in front of her, and looked into her face. 'Nasty bruise you've got there?' There was a question in his voice.

She laughed. 'If I were one of my kids I'd tell you how I fell against a door. To be truthful it's a by-product of a meeting I had with one of the parents.'

'Tough lot you have to deal with, for—'

She interrupted him to stop his saying how young she was. 'They've got a tough life to deal with themselves, down at Siskin.'

'That's no excuse for things like this…'

'I never said it was. Now, are you going to take me round to James' house?'

Her voice was bright, her demeanour relaxed, even confident. She was good at putting on a show when it suited her. She'd done it from the first terrifying day she had been stuck in front of a class. One tutor had told her that all teaching was a kind of theatre. More and more she was finding it to be true. Sometimes it was a comedy. But this situation was most like the first act of some tragedy, underscored by a comedy which gave rise to a terrifying desire to laugh.

The mere sight of the policeman opening the police car door for her, with his white shirt gleaming, made her want to laugh uproariously; as did the stolid presence of the uniformed driver in the front of the car; as did the glimpse of her mother peering through the curtains as she raced away at top speed, to talk to James Denton whose little brothers had just been murdered.

CHAPTER TWELVE

FIRES

The Denton house was on one of the narrow streets climbing up the hill halfway between the school and the Old Baths. Saunders dropped Rachel at the end of the street where James lived.

'Just talk to him,' he said. 'Get him to talk. Then maybe when he starts talking to you, he'll end up talking to us. Just ignore the gaggle of reporters.'

She knocked on the door, which fronted straight onto the street. It was a full minute before it was opened by a fair plump girl in her mid-teens who looked at her mildly enough, but said nothing.

'I'm James' teacher. I wondered how he

was.'

The girl nodded and turned round to walk down the long passage. Rachel followed her, assuming that was what was indicated. The long passage led into a large front room, buried in a muddy brown daytime-twilight caused by the drawn curtains.

The girl led through to a back room which was a kind of living-kitchen. It was warm. A big coal fire burned in the cream enamel fireplace with its side oven. Rachel could smell something baking. A twintub washer was churning away noisily, and a small fat woman, with grey hair threaded through the gold, had just hoisted a washing-basket onto her hip, obviously about to go outside to peg the washing on the line. She put down her basket and faced Rachel, a flicker of fear in her eyes.

'It's Jimmy's teacher, Mam,' said the girl.

'I thought I might talk to him ...' Rachel looked around the room again, wondering where he was.

The woman watched her face. 'Seems a bit funny, does it ... me washing, baking? Time like this? Well, I've got 'em all to care for. All of 'em. Two of mine and two of his. Jonno and Mikey, like, they were the ones my man and I had together ...'

Mrs Davis kicked the basket so it moved along the floor and felt in her apron pocket for a cigarette packet. She offered one to Rachel which she refused. She lit one for herself, then picked up the basket again. 'Well, I'd better get these out. This rain should stop in a while. Our Jimmy's sitting on a wall out the back. Never said nowt since they brought him home. Won't talk to no one.'

James' broad face turned deep red when he saw Rachel and scrambled down from his perch on the wall. 'Hello James. I was wondering where you were.'

He turned his head awkwardly to one side and watched his mother hanging washing out in the drizzle.

'What about a walk? Can I take him for a walk, Mrs Davis? Up to the recreation ground?'

'All right with me. He needs to get away from this place. We all do. He'll need his jacket. Go and get it, Jimmy.'

The mother stood watching him as he went inside. 'Good boy, he is. I've seen that policeman watching him. But our Jimmy couldn't harm a fly. Real innocent. Our Jonno and Mikey used to look out for him. How will he manage now?'

Rachel took a step towards her, but she had started to peg out the clothes again, the drizzle mixing with tears on her face.

James came back out with his parka on, its hood down. Rachel put out her hand for him and he took it. His hand was larger than hers and sticky with wet rain.

He kept his head down as they walked along

164

and she respected his silence till they were sitting on the bench in the middle of the bandstand. From here they could see the green of the recreation ground against the background of the streets on all four sides. 'Good views from here, James. We can see a long way.'

He nodded, pushing his shoe over the crumbling concrete under his foot.

'You didn't half like doing your rubbings last week, isn't that right, James?'

This time he looked at her when he nodded.

'Shall we do some more some day? In the woods?'

He looked at her. 'I can do it. I'm good at that.'

'Yes you are, James.'

'I was telling Mikey and Jonno that I was good at it.'

'Were you?'

'They didn't come home. They went, and they didn't come home. Our Mikey and Jonno.'

There was a long silence. The drizzle had stopped for the moment, but the water continued to drip down the dome of the bandstand and off its rusty piecrust edge.

'They went there, Miss. To where I done them. The rubbings.'

'They went there,' she repeated. 'I heard they went there, to the Old Baths.'

'Yes. Three times. Only the last time...'

165

'Three times? Why did they go back?'

'They was playing a game, Miss. Islands. Our Jonno said it was a brahma game.'

'Whose game was it? Did Jonno make it up?'

'Nah. Too little. Their mate made it. He was bigger.'

Rachel took her gaze away from James, and watched the rain dripping from the rusty iron. She tried to keep her voice light. 'Whose game, James? Who made the game?'

'I'm not to tell you. Making trouble for Jonno and Mikey. Said it was secret. I wanted a go, the last time, Sunday afternoon, but he wouldn't let me. Jonno and Mikey ran away from there. He said they were bad lads. But I'm not to tell.'

'You could tell me, Jimmy. I'm sure it wouldn't count if you told me.' She paused. 'He meant the other kids. He didn't want them to spoil it. The game.'

James nodded. 'He said it, that. But Mikey and Jonno went back, and look what the bad man did. My Mam says did I see the bad man. But I seen no bad man.' He shook his head and started shivering.

Rachel put an arm out and pulled him beside her and rubbed his large hands. 'It's cold here James. We should go back.'

He turned his head to look at her. 'He's good, that Ian, isn't he, Miss? He knows about the things. How you should go on, like. He liked my rubbing. He knew I could do that,

Ian. Our Jonno liked Ian. He had chocolate.'

They walked back slowly, Rachel forcing herself not to race. At first they walked separately on the pavement, two feet between them. Then James came and slipped his hand in hers.

Back at the house, Mrs Davis insisted on giving Rachel a scone fresh from the oven, and a cup of tea. She talked about Jonathan and Michael and showed Rachel a photograph of them at the seaside with their buckets and spades. On a daytrip, she said. Funnily enough on that daytrip it had been really hot. All day. It had been a change. Usually on daytrips it rained.

There was no sign of Saunders' car when she got out of the house so she fought her way silently through the reporters, refusing to answer any questions, then she walked slowly all the way home, her mind tumbling around, up and down, back and forward. She would telephone Saunders. James had got it jumbled up, confusing the times he had been at the Baths. How much use this would be to Saunders she couldn't think. She'd ring him, when she got home.

* * *

Saunders looked down at the shredded, charred remains of the clothes, made soft and pulpy by the day's rain. The same rain had

167

given the hard mud surface of the clearing a rime of black scum.

His colleague had laid out the clothes—the remains of a T-shirt, a jumper and pale blue trousers—on a white plastic sheet. Keeping one hand in his pocket, he turned the fragments over with his pen. There were brown spots and specks on each piece. The neckband of the T-shirt was still complete. He turned it over. There was a neatly embroidered name. He pursed his lips with some satisfaction.

He walked back to the edge of the clearing and looked back at the pathetic scraps as they lay on the white sheet. Backing up like this, he nearly tripped over a stone, jammed upright in the rising bank. The remains of the hasty bonfire were just in front of it.

He looked around. The police photographer was still busy. The two police cars were up on the road, with one or two press cars behind, and a buzzing ripple of watchers kept back by a ribbon barrier and a watchful policeman.

He squatted down and fingered the stone, then pulled his fingers away to note the fine film of soot. He called across to the constable who was standing, feet apart, beside the white plastic sheet. 'I need some paper. Have you got some paper?'

The young man looked puzzled, and pulled out his notebook.

'No. Bigger than that. Go down to the school and ask for some. Drawing paper. That would do.'

The constable was back in ten minutes, with three sheets of drawing paper. He handed one to Saunders. 'What's it for, sir?'

'I'm gonna do a rubbing.' Saunders kneeled down in the mud and smoothed the paper flat over the stone. Then he rubbed the heel of his hand and the tips of his fingers right across it, rubbing closely. He peeled the damp paper off and stood up, holding it up to the light. 'Here, son, what do you see?'

'A dirty bit of paper, sir.'

'Look again.'

'Nowt, sir. A paper all covered with soot from that fire.'

'No face?'

'No face, sir.'

He put the sheet between the two other sheets, and told the constable to put them in the car, along with the charred clothes. He rubbed his hands together to dry them from the damp paper, looked round and shivered. He had been in some bad places and this was definitely one of them.

'Some business, this,' he said, to nobody in particular.

*   *   *

Ian didn't bother to go to school on the Tuesday. His Nana was still in heavy slumber when he came downstairs; he could hear the faint rattle of her snore. He had heard her coming in the previous night, chattering away and talking to herself like she did when she was drunk. He'd put his head under his blanket, hoping she wouldn't come in to check on him. The bedroom door did creak, but he lay very still. It creaked again and clicked shut.

On his way downstairs he looked into Sandra's room and saw the bed, neatly made, smooth and cold. He went into the room and carefully pulled open the bottom drawer of her large chest. He found the red sweater Maureen had worn the day before. He pulled it over his head, taking in Sandra's scent as it came over his face. He stood in front of the mirror pulling his hands down the soft wool from his shoulders to his waist. Then he pushed the wide sleeves up his arms. It was loose and large on him, but he felt good.

He went downstairs and opened the fridge. There wasn't much inside. He took out a slightly rusty half-empty tin of pineapples and one of peaches, and tipped them into the large bowl that Maureen had used the night before to put the chips in, as she cut them. He stood on a chair and took a tin of Carnation evaporated milk out of a cupboard over the sink. He punched two holes in it and poured the lot on top of the orange and yellow mound of fruit.

He sat in the smallest easy chair with the big bowl on his knee, and ate very slowly, relishing every mouthful.

Feeling full of sweet things, he made his way to the Old Baths. The rainy drizzle was making diamond glitters on the hairy surface of the red jumper. A single police car stood outside the Baths with a man in uniform leaning down to talk to the driver inside. A small group of women hovered, and a young man in jeans and a T-shirt was waiting beside the car, trying to say something to the policeman.

Ian walked along to a piece of fencing away from the gate and peered through. Two more policemen were inside poking at the stones. The places where Jonno and Mikey had lain were still marked with tape stretched between sticks on the lumpy ground.

'Hey, what're you doin', what's yer name?' The policeman beside the car was calling to him. He ran his very hardest, and finally escaped the pounding feet in the backstreets. Then he made his way through the town up to the Old Cross. The boy. Maybe he would be there.

He was surprised when he saw the police cars and the people, and the whole corner cordoned off with red tape. He pushed his way between two women and looked across to the clearing where he had first seen the boy. There were more policeman there, including the thick-set square-faced one who had asked all the questions and had come to the house. The hood of the man's anorak was pulled up against the drizzle and he had one hand pushed

171

deep into his pocket. With the other he was picking away with a biro at the fragments of cloth which were the only remains of the clothes that Ian had worn twice. They hadn't burned properly. He should have stayed to check.

Ian watched as the policeman peered closer at one of the fragments, then nodded and said something. Then he was bending down at the stone where Jimmy Denton had made his rubbing. Ian decided that this was no place for him. He needed to be away.

Standing inside the doorway of his own house, he listened carefully. Not a sound. No noise at all. So he set to work.

He piled up the last scraps of his comics in the cupboard where the clothes had lain. Then he took one from the top of the pile and twisted it into a torch. He carefully lit this with Maureen's cigarette lighter and set fire to the rest of the comics. Then he set fire to her copy of the *Daily Mirror* where it lay on the table, showing pictures of Mikey and Jonno. Then he held the torch under the curtains in the sitting room and in the kitchen till they were smoking, and one or two licks of flame were curling up. The two rooms were filling with smoke and flames now. He watched for a moment then opened the back door and fled down the back street. The rain had stopped and he felt warm; quite hot. He thought about taking off the red jumper, but decided against it.

When Rachel finally reached home, Ian was sitting crouched on her doorstep like a little red gnome. She thought of Maureen Sobell leaping onto her last night in the hall. She was visited by yet another desire to laugh out loud. This, she gulped back, is silly. Stop it. She looked quickly to the bay window for her mother's face, ever watchful, through the curtains.

'No one here,' said Ian. 'She's gone. I waited down at the corner, and she went out. To the bus stop. She got a bus.'

'What do you want?'

His face was smudged with black, his hair was greasy and lank, falling down onto the unlikely red jumper. The silver-rimmed eyes looking up into hers appeared to have black lines drawn round them. He tried using his will on her. She had to be on his side. 'My ... my foot's hurting again, Miss. I thought you might maybe put some more of that stuff on it.'

His foot? She had forgotten about the foot. Her mind was whirling with this other thing. She had to telephone Saunders. 'Ian, James Denton says you made the game...'

'What game was that, Miss?'

She sighed. 'He can get muddled, James, but I'm sure ... Did you know your Nana came to see me last night?'

'No, Miss.' She put her key in the lock and ushered him into the kitchen. 'Just sit there. I

173

have to make a phone call.'

Saunders wasn't there, so she left a message for him to telephone.

The two of them were silent together as she repeated the routine of washing the foot and dressing it. It was much improved; hardly any swelling at all. 'It's much better, Ian. Can't be hurting you that much.'

'Are you getting that copper here, Miss?'

'Yes.'

'Why?'

'Because I have something to tell him.'

'What'll you tell him?'

'That's my business.'

He watched her with his light eyes, clinging to the stool as though he expected her to pull him off.

'Come on, Ian. What are you playing at? What about what James says? Did you see Michael and Jonathan on Sunday?'

'I need to go home, Miss, but I can't.'

'Why not?'

'I made a fire. In a cupboard. My Nana'll kill us if I go back. She'll murder us.'

Rachel sighed. 'Look, I'll just wait for this call, then I'll come across to Siskin with you.'

'I can't go, Miss. She'll put us in a cage. They'll put us in a cage.' He was wailing now with his mouth wide open, his eyes red and tearless.

'What are you saying, Ian? Don't be silly.'

The doorbell gave two long rings, vibrating

urgency through the house. She put her hands on his shoulders and looked at him. 'Now shut up and sit there.'

Saunders bustled after her into the sitting room. 'You needn't have come, Mr Saunders. I just asked for you to ring. Just an idea I had. I talked to James Denton. He was very confused.'

'I was coming here anyway, Miss Waterman.' He lingered over the name. 'Anyway, did you get the lad to say anything?'

'Eventually. He said there was a game. Islands. I've played it myself, many times. When I was small. And he said the game was made by another child. Just children's games, Mr Saunders. I can't believe.' ... She paused, then spoke with great care. 'I can't imagine ... Not that that means ...'

'At the very least, Miss Waterman, it means we have to find that child; talk to him ... Or her. It could be a her.' He thought of the clothes.

'Could it? Yes. I suppose so.'

He opened his battered briefcase. He pulled out two clear plastic bags, and flattened them out on the coffee table. 'I wondered, Miss Waterman, if you could tell me anything about these?'

She turned them over and over. They were fragments, but she knew what they were. Heavy grey lead was creeping into the crannies inside her. 'Yes I can. They're clothes of my sister's. That's her name. I gave them to a child about a week ago. There had been an accident. He'd hurt his foot. Who burnt them? What are those marks?'

'The marks are blood. And we thought you might be able to tell us who burnt them. Who is this child?'

'Ian Sobell. He's here, in the kitchen. You see, he's had this little accident at home and he's frightened of his...' She was walking along the hall.

The kitchen was empty.

'Scarpered.' He looked at her, a thread of excitement in his voice. 'Well we're gonna have to talk to his people, anyway, now. The mother's away. She's known to us. Keeps bad company. It's the grandmother, isn't it, who takes care of the lad?'

Rachel touched her face, making the bruise hurt more. 'Can I come with you? If he is there, he'll need someone. This accident, Mr Saunders. He said he had set fire to a cupboard. Set fire to the house.'

'Jesus!'

They arrived just as the firefighters were winding up their gear. The windows of the house were like blackened eyeholes; burnmarks crept right up the walls like finger marks. Some firemen were still inside the house, throwing the smouldering refuse out of the windows. An ambulance had just pulled away, its bells danging.

The street was crowded with people. There were reporters with cameras. Rachel thought it was like a re-run of the scene at the school gates on Monday morning. The nervous smile was pushing itself out of her lips again. She scanned the crowd. At the very far end of the clutch of people she saw the figure with the loose and floppy red jumper.

She walked towards him and put out her hand, palm up.

'Ian . . .' she said.

PART TWO

IN TRANSIT

Tread on a line
Your mother's kind
Tread on squares, your mother
swears.

(For saying...)

CHAPTER THIRTEEN

VISITING TIME

1966

The walls of the dayroom were twenty feet high; the windows too vast to be curtained, but down here below Rachel noted some attempts to make the scale more domestic; the feeling personal. Tables and chairs were set around in groups. The table before her had a pile of *Woman's Weeklies*, which she regularly tried and failed to read. The table by the clinic had a tank with a fish swimming in it. Two fish had swum there last week. However one had been eaten in a slice of bread by a patient called Mary Ann. Mary Ann was on a vendetta against a night sister, who spoke to the fishes every day and whom Mary Ann considered to be quite mad.

Rachel had discussed the affair with her favourite nurse Mrs Eltringham, an intelligent middle-aged woman with very fine eyes. Mrs Eltringham often came to sit with Rachel after her work was done, a cause for some jealousy among longer-term patients who considered Eltringham their property. In this hospital nurses were called by their surnames only, both by patients and other staff, a habit Rachel previously assumed only commonplace in the army and boys' schools.

'Of course, Mary Ann's right,' said Eltringham calmly. 'Not much to choose between some of the staff here and the long term patients. We're all institutionalised.'

Rachel eyed her curiously. 'Do you mind that?'

Eltringham shrugged. 'I meet people every day, on the bus, or at the Co-op, who're dafter than people here. And all institutionalised one way or another.'

'So why are the people here?'

'These certain ones've been here for a very long time. Put in for having a baby early, or having some great paddy when they were young, and seemed to have stayed. Institutionalised, like I say.'

'Will that happen to me?' Rachel asked the question humbly enough.

Eltringham smiled briefly and shook her head. 'All you needed was a good rest and an excuse to do nothing for six months. To let your soul catch up with your body, as my sister would say.'

'What about all these pills and all this talking that people are making me do?'

'I'm sure they must be doing you a bit of good,' said Eltringham firmly. 'But it's the rest that'll make the difference. Seen it time and time again. Sleep, knitting the ravelled sleeve of care, as the bard says.'

'And what about Mr Barlow's having me burble on and on?' Rachel was beginning to dread the little talks with Mr Barlow who seemed to walk her round in spongy circles and get her no further forward. 'Always mother-mother-mothering...'

Eltringham patted her arm. 'That's all right dear. If you came in with varicose veins he'd have you talking about your mother. To be honest, though, in your case, I'd 'a thought you...'

'That's what I'm in for?' The savage dreams were about her mother, who had died very suddenly on Christmas Eve, striking her with a depth of terror like a sour core deep within her. Barlow was trying to talk to her about guilt. 'I keep trying to tell him I don't feel guilty at my mother dying, I feel guilty at not being sadder when she died, but...'

After the funeral she had started wandering around the town in her nightie, a habit which had culminated in a rather undignified chase involving her, the ghost of mother, Elena and the doctor, which had ended up in the middle of a farmer's field with a rather restive bull.

And then there were the screams, the dreadful screams, that only she could hear. 'He tries to get me to talk about things which happened before, which mean nothing, nothing to me...' Her voice rose, and Eltringham put a firm hand on her forearm.

'Steady on love,' she soothed.

'Can I tell you something terrible?' said Rachel cautiously.

'Only if you need to,' said Eltringham.

'That Mr Barlow. I feel a bit like Mary Ann over him. I think he's mad. I know for certain he's madder than I'll ever be. Mother, mother mothering, he's obsessed with mothers. His mother must have dropped him on his head when he was a baby.'

Eltringham smiled slightly. 'Well, love, if he's mad he's in the right place, like us all, isn't he?' She stood up and lifted her fob watch which was lying on her capacious bosom. 'Time for your tablets, love.'

Rachel stood up, tied the cord of her dressing gown and walked along with her to the clinic. 'Have you a family, Nurse Eltringham?'

'Four. Brought them up on my own. I'd be a very great disappointment to Mr Barlow, I'm afraid … Never had much time to do the motherly things.'

'What do they do? Your children?'

'Two work in a factory, one's at college, and the other's at school.'

'You must be proud of them.'

Eltringham shrugged. 'We all love our own,' she said.

She handed Rachel her tablets and watched her swallow them. 'There's a woman you might like; a psychiatrist. I think you might like her. She's very practical. Not airy-fairy like these men here. Maybe you should ask for her. Her name's Daisy Montague.'

*　　*　　*

'My, you've grown!' Maureen looked at the tall boy sitting on the hard chair opposite. Short glow-white hair, combed forward. Pale gleaming grey eyes. She glanced away from those eyes, her gaze fixing on a triangular dried flower arrangement in the tall fireplace.

His lips carved themselves into a smile. 'Three years on, Nana, three meals a day, training twice a week; it makes a difference.' His voice was deeper too.

She stirred uneasily in her chair, wondering why on earth she'd come. Oh, yes, that letter had come, in such a flowing, confident hand.

Reg had come upon the letter as he was raking around for a comb on the mantelpiece. Reg liked to go home tidy. 'Seems a reasonable sort of letter, Mo. You should go and see him. Tell him about us.' He read the letter aloud. Made her listen.

She had just skimmed through it when it arrived, not wanting to know its contents.

March 16th, 1966.
Dear Nana,
Thank you for the letter. Must be a year since I heard from you. Except for the Christmas card. So it was nice to hear your

news. This is, like you say, a better place to stay even though they still keep a tight watch. There is more to do—workshops and things. I've started some woodwork and have started a 'gen-u-ine' O Level course. If I stay here long enough, I'll be able to take the big exam in two years time. The lads aren't too bad, really. One or two pile it on a bit, and you have to stick up for yourself. It sounds like our Sandra's doing all right down in London. Like you say, she only needs a decent chance and that job in the club should keep the wolf from the door. And fancy you having a job in a factory! Sounds all right, really. At least you can sit down at the machines. And, like you say, it's company. Maybe, with those wages, you'll be able to save up and come down here to visit one month. Anyway, when you write to Sandra, give her my best. If you could let me have her address, I will write to her.

All the best, your grandson,
Ian.

Ian met her gaze, bringing her back to the present. 'And I run every day. There's an all-weather track here.'

She turned her head to survey the room, with its wood panelling and arched, stone-traced windows. 'These places are pretty good these days.'

The grey eyes sparked. 'Don't start telling

186

me it's better than Butlins. I read those letters in the papers every day. Letters! People like us shouldn't have television. And we drink wine with our meals; we have room-service, have you heard? We should be locked away, the key thrown in the canal; barbed wire on the window-ledges...'

'I didn't say—'

'The other place; that'd've suited you better. Not dark, mind you. Really bright lights. More like a hospital. No nooks and crannies to hide in. High window-ledges, hard surfaces. Nothing to pick up. Nothing to harm yourself with. Or anybody else.'

'I saw that place. You wouldn't know that, because when I got round to going there, you'd gone onto the next place.' She rooted around in her bag and pulled out a chunky block of Cadbury's Fruit & Nut and a packet of twenty Benson & Hedges cigarettes.

He lifted the gold pack and pushed it towards her. 'I don't smoke,' he said.

She looked round the room. 'I thought. Someone said...'

'Neither do I let anybody else do it where I am.' He put his head on one side. 'You've had your hair cut.'

She patted the neat short hair behind her ears, sitting up straight. 'New perm. Had it done specially to come down here. Like this it's better, for getting up for work and things. You don't have the time, do you?'

'I don't know. I have lots of time,' he said. 'Don't you?'

She clenched her fists. The times she would have given him a good belting for just such a veiled cheeky look. She sat remembering the smoke, then blackness, then no air at all to breathe. Then waking up in hospital with the policemen and all those other people talking to her. What they were suggesting was ridiculous. Of course, they got on like a house on fire, she and Ian. She had actually used those words and her questioners exchanged glances. They were everything to each other. Sure he was naughty. Often played with matches and fire. Banned him from the house, hadn't she? Saved him from himself many a time. Anyway, he wouldn't realise she was in the house, would he, that she was there? Would he?

'What're you thinking, Nana?'

'I was wondering whether you knew I was there. That day. Whether you really knew.' She paused. 'The fire, that didn't bother me. You'd always been a troublesome little bugger. And I got me new house out of it, away from Siskin. But setting fire to it with me there, in bed?' She leaned forward, her neck right out of her collar. 'Ian?'

He let a long pause melt its way through the room, along the carpet, up the curtains and vanish into the high stone windows. A frown etched itself onto his smooth white brow. 'I've thought about it a lot, time to time. They used to ask me a lot about that, early days. Some of them were nutters themselves, those shrinks. Made out I was listening to voices. Did I think I was hearing the Devil, they said. Nutters. But one or two, they made a bit of sense. In some ways I had reason to do something, the way you ... were on with me. But I don't think I did it to you. What I really wanted to do was to burn the house. I was keen to do that. I can remember that. The other I couldn't remember. Nothing else.'

She sat back more easily in her chair. 'I said that. I said, no way would you mean it. We were everything to each other, you and me.'

He raised a silvery brow. 'Everything, Nana? A letter a year and a single visit in three years. Everything?'

'I was in hospital, remember. A long time. I did come twice, to that first place. Bloody waste of time. Said you wouldn't ... couldn't see me the first time. Then they'd moved you without telling me. Then, time flies by, pet. Life goes on. And I've got work now. And friends. And here you are at the other end of the country nearly.'

'Friends? You have friends?'

She went red. 'Well I've got this man friend now. Reg Godwit. A line-leader at work. Good feller. Good worker. He drove me down here, it being factory fortnight. Said I should tell you.'

'Tell me what?'

'Well, I'm moving in with him. We'll get

married in December. It'll be a Christmas wedding.'

'How nice!' He leaned swiftly towards her. She flinched. He kissed her on the cheek. 'Mrs Godwit, will it be? And will you wear a big white frock, at this Christmas wedding?'

'Sarky bugger. You always were sarky. Out of the corner of your eyes. Always sarky.'

'So you're moving?'

She pushed a scrap of paper across at him. 'This is the address. Reg, he has this house up at High Ridge. It was his mother's. And then she passed on. So...'

'So you're changing your name. Maureen Godwit. Has a ring that! Our Sandra, she married that feller in London. You wrote that in last year's letter, didn't you? Soon there'll be no Sobell left. No bad thing.'

'There's you.'

'Me? If ... when ... I get out, I'll change my name. It's done nowt for me, spread across the papers for years.'

She was curious. 'What'll you call yourself?'

'There's an old feller, been coming to see me since that second place. Bit of a do-gooder but he's all right. Escaped from the Nazis in the last war. Tells great stories. I asked him once if I could use his name. He said he wouldn't mind. No kids, see? Because of the war. He has a good name.'

'What name would that be then?' asked Maureen eagerly.

190

He shook his head slowly. 'Think I'd tell you?' he said softly. 'No chance. Hard up for a week, and you'd be selling it to the *News of the World*. But thanks anyway.'

'What for?'

'For not vanishing entirely without trace. A letter a year and one visit isn't much, but it's something.'

She shook her head. 'It's hardened you. Hardened you, being in here.'

He laughed out loud at this. 'Here long enough and I'll be hard as rock, right through.'

'Don't they say? Don't they know? How long?'

'There's reviews and things. And I've been as good as gold in here. I've been a very good boy. All the time. Play the game by their rules. People outside, though . . .'

'The papers. You should see the papers sometimes. Raking it up, just when everything settles down. I said then, and've said ever since, an accident. That's all it was. Do you . . . They say you don't remember.'

He shrugged. 'They say so, so I must have done it. But . . . anyway, Nana, I think I've worked that out. Like I said, I've had help here, and in the other places. I think I know what happened now . . . the pressure I was under . . . me living in my own world. And that there's fault around and it's not all mine. They helped me see why it happened, to make me remember. But I still can't . . .'

'Why? Why? I could never understand. Why? Why you'd set fire to the house, why you'd...'

He leaned back, looking her in the eyes.

She sat up straight again and returned him look for look. 'I'll tell you whose fault it was. That loopy teacher you had then.'

'Teacher?'

'That Waterman woman. She started it all off.'

'Don't talk junk.'

'Junk, is it? She's ended up in the loony bin anyway. Doesn't that show? Been in Lunton Hospital six months to my knowledge.'

He frowned. 'Six months? Lunton?'

'She tossed her loop altogether when that old bag died. You know, the mother? Well, that was because of the papers as well. Just before last Christmas. Another one of these true life stories with you at the centre playing the child-devil. I got so mad! So I goes down there; takes the paper to show the Waterman woman what she had started. Just what it was she'd done done to me, like. Well, the old bag had hysterics...' She smiled up at him. 'I showed'm, see. The old bag was dead next day. And the lass went off her head. Off to the loony bin eventually.' There was satisfaction in her smile.

'You wreak havoc wherever you go, you...' He was standing up, moving round to her side

192

of the table. The man lounging in the corner straightened up. Ian put his hands gently on her shoulders. 'Time to go, Nana.'

She looked round the room. 'Who says?'

'I say.'

She stood up, throwing off his restraining hands. He shrugged. 'Well, Reg'll be waiting for me. We're going to have a run down to the coast, after.' She pulled her scarf round her neat perm and stood up.

He held himself stiff, away from her so she couldn't attempt to kiss him, as she had when she arrived.

'Well, love. Nice to see you looking so well.'

'Have a nice time at the coast.'

'Yes. We'll do that.'

He watched her go out of her door.

'Nana?'

'Yes love?'

'That perm?'

'Yes love?'

'It puts years on you.'

He caught one glance of the old familiar rage before the man closed the door firmly after her, then came across to pick up the chocolate bar. 'Ian! You left your chocolate!'

'You keep it Mr MacIntire. You can have it. I don't want it. I never did like chocolate.'

Back in his narrow room he laid out his pen and notepad in neat order on the little table and sat down to write in his neat flowing hand.

July 23rd, 1966.

Dear Miss Waterman,

I was wondering how you were. My Nana visited here and said it had been in the papers that you'd been ill at Christmastime. So I wondered how you were. They will miss you at school as you were the only teacher who was worth anything. I'm in a different place than when I wrote to you last year. This is a big house set in all these grounds. There is an outdoor running track and a sports hall. I do work-outs in there as it is useful to be strong. There are workshops and a whole school block. Really, school is better than before, because if anything, it breaks the boredom here. I'll be doing some exams the year after next, if I stick in. And I'm doing some wood-carving, although I'm only supposed to do that under supervision because of the tools. They had to have a special meeting because of the knife. We use mostly Balsa wood. Did you know there is a wood called quick-wood which is the dead wood from a tree which has been struck by lightning? I'd like to carve some of that. I do claywork as well; building on instead of gouging out. The teacher who comes for claywork reminds me of you. She is tall and wears these smock things. I had a letter from my Nana and she said our Sandra is married now and working in clubs in London. One big chance and she'll make it. It's a sure thing. Hoping you are keeping well now, and your sister.

Yours sincerely, Ian Sobell

PS. I didn't hear whether or not you got my last letter. PPS I have started this carving that I'll give to you one day.

CHAPTER FOURTEEN

COMMUNICATIONS

'Elena? Elena? Is it you?'

'God, who's this?' The voice at the other end of the line was suddenly swallowed by a yawn.

'Oh, no! I've woken you up! You're on nights. I forgot. I'll ring back. Really. I'll ring back.'

'Don't talk stupid, Rache. I'm up now, woken up. Look I'm sitting up. Now what is it? What can I do for you?'

'I wondered how you were.'

'I'm fine. Nights wreak havoc with your social life, don't they? But apart from that it's fine. The sister I'm with on this turn is even vaguely human. More important, how are you?'

'All right. Much better. Steadier all together. I'm off most of the pills now, but I still go to the hospital, seeing my ... psychiatrist, counsellor ... whatever.'

'Does that make a difference?'

'She's a help; she listens a lot and talks

common sense. Like brushing away bogey men with a dust-pan and brush and a dab of Dettol.' Rachel laughed. 'I sometimes think our meeting makes her happy.'

'Oh, Rache, that's more like it; more like your old self.' Elena paused. Rachel could hear her shuffle around in bed as she sat up straighter. 'Do you know, I've felt so awful coming away, even enjoying it, while you've been going through all this.'

'Listen, love, even as I plodged through the foggiest of fogs you were the bright spark. You across there in Manchester doing just what was right for you. I wanted it. I wanted you to get away.'

'Good egg. So what is it, kiddo? What made you lift the dreaded phone?'

It had been a major symptom: not being able to lift the phone; panicking at the thought of such an action. Terrified each time it rang. And the car. Finding herself up strange alleyways and wondering how she had driven there. Then wild panics, even as she got into the car. Then not being able to drive at all. That had started even before her mother died just after the events at the Old Baths. She had never driven since then. It was as though the bit of her brain which knew how to drive had been wiped out of her head.

She put the phone to her other ear. 'I had a letter, Ellie. From Ian Sobell.'

There was a long silence, then a hard voice.

'They shouldn't allow it. How could they? That potty grandmother of his pursuing you last year.' She paused, and in the silence between them was the raging storm in the house which had brought on their mother's last attack.

'You can't blame him for his potty grandmother. You might blame her for him. Anyway, I don't think it is allowed. He's managed to get letters posted somehow. There must be ways. It's all right, Ellie. A nice letter. Couldn't be more ordinary.'

'Mmm.'

'He seems to be getting on quite well.'

'Mmm.'

'He mentions another letter. Last year. Was there another letter?'

'Yes. One came. We...'

'We...'

'Me and Ma ... For once I agreed with the old boot.'

'What?'

'Don't shout, Rache! Listen. Listen to me. You didn't know whether you were coming or going, even then. Didn't know whether you were on your ace or your apex. Hanging on by a thread. So we...'

'Where is it?'

'The letter? Somewhere. I'm sure she wouldn't have destroyed it. But I can't say where...'

'Right, thanks. I'll look for it.'

Rachel put down the phone and looked

around the cluttered sitting room. Then she went into the kitchen and pulled out a roll of black plastic bags from the cupboard under the sink.

Back in the sitting room she set to work. By teatime she had ten bulging black sacks in line outside the back door. In them were all the nicknacks, magazines, bits of paper and sentimental pictures which marked her mother's reign in the house. There were obsolete spectacles and corsets, hoarded against some day which never came. There were best dresses and trim suits only barely worn; leather gloves and a neat, belted mackintosh. And four tins of Lavendo Polish, left from a box of six her mother bought for economy.

By the time Rachel was finished the house was stripped bare of all visible evidence of her mother's presence. She retained only two things: one was some half-done needlepoint which depicted a bowl of fruit; a present from Rachel herself, which her mother had abandoned after filling one section of the pomegranate, muttering about the ugliness of modern designs and modern colours. The other was the letter to her, unread, from Ian Sobell.

Rachel laid the needlepoint on the table under the sitting room window, with the letter and today's letter beside it. The one she had received this morning was on the left; the other, written the previous summer, before the most recent cataclysm in her life, was on the right. Beside them was her own letter-pad, her ink-bottle and her fountain pen. She poured herself a generous gin and tonic (her first since she had stopped taking the pills), and sat down to write.

Dear Ian,

It was a real surprise to get your letter. In fact I had to read two at once, as I've been away, you see, so I didn't actually read the first one till very recently. I have been in a hospital. I was ill for six months. More than that. You see, my mother died just before Christmas and the strain of this made me quite ill.

It was very strange in hospital. The routine was very strong and I seemed to sleep a great deal. The days and weeks seemed both very long and very short. What you said in your first letter reminded me of that.

From your two letters it seems that your present place is rather nicer than your last place. Plenty to do. It is good that you're finding so much to do. I can tell from your letter how well your English is coming on. And the woodwork and claywork can be very absorbing, as I know. When I was in hospital I did a lot of painting. I found it very absorbing and it took me out of the closed hospital world. I am going to put some of my pictures on the walls of my house. I have just been clearing some space for them this morning.

It must be nice to feel a bit more settled now and getting to know people a little better, although I imagine some people are passing through rather than staying. Anyway, stick to your studies Ian. You have a brain and should use it. You're a clever person, and using that cleverness on your studies will be a great resource for the future.

I am not yet back at school, but will do some part-time teaching next term, then in January will go to a brand new school at Low Ridge.

Thank you for asking about my sister. She has finished school now, of course, and is in Manchester training to be a nurse. She seems well set for a good career in nursing.

Best wishes, and as I say, stick to your studies.

R Waterman.

'Rache?'

'Oh! Hello Elena!'

'Are you all right? I couldn't sleep all day for thinking about you.'

'I'm fine.'

'Are you sure? That stupid boy writing to you...'

'I'm fine. Really, Elena. They're only simple

letters from a young lad who's stuck...'

'Ordinary? You must be joking. You've seen all the stuff in the papers about him.'

'Papers. Suddenly Ellie, you sound like Ma. I'd watch that if I were you. Now just go to work; tie some bandages and calm down.' Rachel put down the phone with a very satisfying and very neat click.

1st June, 1967.

Dear Miss Waterman,

I hear from the adviser, Mr Thrush, that you are out of hospital and feeling much better. And that, with great courage you have decided not to take a breakdown pension but to work as supernumary teacher at Low Ridge Primary School. For personal reasons I am very sorry you have decided not to return here in September. I do, however understand that you wish to make a new start. In some ways now this is such a sad school. First Miss Rawlings went on sick leave never to return. And we have been made sadder now by your absence. Then there is the perpetual talk of the demolition of Siskin and our school with it. The seeds which sprouted forth in those terrible events five years ago are still lying dormant here. One's best prayer is that they may remain dormant. All else is beyond our power.

So, our loss is Low Ridge's gain. Although you and I, perhaps, have not seen eye to eye over methods and approaches, your work gained great respect here, in regard to your understanding of the children and their needs and in regard to the humour and conscientiousness of your approach to your professional task. My particular respect for you doubled when I saw how you buckled down to work after those terrible events, despite the obvious strain under which you laboured.

As to the future, remember Henley's words:

> Out of the night that covers me,
> Black as the Pit from pole to pole,
> I thank whatever gods may be
> For my unconquerable soul
>
> In the fell clutch of circumstance,
> I have not winced nor cried aloud;
> Under the bludgeonings of chance
> My head is bloody, but unbowed...
>
> ... It matters not how strait the gate,
> How charged with punishments the scroll,
> I am the master of my fate:
> I am the captain of my soul.

(Perhaps, knowing your strong views on the subject, I should have written here 'mistress' of fate. However, as you well know, I am more comfortable with the old usage.) God

bless and help you,
    Sincerely,
        Keith Warner.

8th July, 1967
  Well, Dearie!
  Good to hear that you're back in the land
of the living! Old Warner says you'll be
teaching at my end of the town in
September. Low Ridge Primary School!
Now there's posh! Plate glass windows and
docile seven year olds. So our paths will
cross unseen every day, old love. Me coming
across there to work; you coming across here
to work. You'll have them all reading
Shakespeare in no time, which will suit the
parents round here, who have what the
Guardian calls 'high aspirations' for their
children. Trouble is, they all think their
children should be doctors and lawyers, even
if their brains are of the two-short-planks
variety.
  Old Warner said he's written to you. Did
he wheel out the one about being 'master of
your soul'??? Joking apart, he's a good
enough sort deep down. Wrote to me after
my dear Emmie died, in those terms. Even as
I laughed, he helped me, somehow. He
means well.
  Now then, to business! I'm sure the Doc
has prescribed lots of fresh air and all that
for your convalescence. How would you like

to watch the greatest village cricket team in the North in a crucial match against its great rival next Saturday? I have it on good authority that it will be brilliantly sunny from dawn till dusk. And there is this very comfortable seat under an old tree. Mind you they say if you go round it seven times in the wrong direction, you see the Devil. So don't do that, as this is a crucial championship match and we need all the support we can get.

If I don't hear from you, I'll call at one fifteen on Saturday and sweep you off.

With best wishes,
Jack Marriott.

'There now, dearie. Are you comfortable? I've got a rug in the car if you want one?'

Rachel laughed. 'Jack! Stoppit! I was in hospital for my head not my body. My body is perfectly all right.'

He hovered around, his uncertainty ludicrous for such a large man. 'Well, dearie, even an old man can see that!'

'Look, Jack. You go over there and discuss the finer points of cricket with your comrades. I'll sit here and do my stitching and read my book.'

His face cleared and he loped off with a springy stride.

She stitched another section of the pomegranate, then put it on her lap and put her head back on the bark and closed her eyes. Her nose wrinkled and a rank smell drifted in front of her. She opened her eyes to see the dirty feet of a boy who was sitting with his back to the side of the tree. She peered across to meet round eyes that seemed to have no iris under a thatch of hair. She smiled faintly. 'Are you enjoying the game?'

He shook his head. Then his jerkinned body seemed to shimmer on the air as she closed her eyes; the smell became stronger. When she opened them, the boy was gone.

She attended a few more end of season matches, and well wrapped up, sat under the same tree, but she never saw the boy again.

*   *   *

In the Autumn, she started to teach in Low Ridge School. With a teacher becoming pregnant she was soon assigned a class of her own and swung again into the compulsive and absorbing rhythms of teaching. She was more like her old self; happy to telephone Elena every week. She went to work on the bus, relieved to find that she was steady enough to enjoy her work. Jack Marriot slipped out of her mind, as did the late summer games of village cricket and the barefoot boy under the tree.

But that was when the dreams began again, and her symptons started to return, and having

205

looked into the abyss of going to hospital or taking the pills again, she hunted out a scrap of paper given to her by Nurse Eltringham, rang the therapist called Daisy Montague and got an appointment within a week.

Having introduced herself, Daisy sat back in her chair, flashed Rachel a brilliant melting smile and said, 'How can I help you Miss Waterman?'

'Have you read my file? You won't want me to go back and tell it all from the beginning. They always want me to go back...'

'It can help...'

'To be perfectly honest I think it helps you lot, not me. It fills the time and makes you feel good.'

Daisy raised her eyebrows. 'Well, Miss Waterman, you've obviously come here for something; why don't you start with your immediate concerns? What's worrying you at the moment?'

'The dreams. There are two. There is this great black void and I am pulled to the centre. And there are bars before me, and I am screaming and in great pain. I shake the bars, and then I can't reach the bars, and I scream. And it only stops when I wake.'

'And the second dream?'

'I am in this terrible place; a place which has high stone columns spaced at regular intervals. The air is all black and there are creepers clinging to the columns.'

206

'Creepers,' said Daisy.

'And I am sometimes jumping from column to column with ease, like a leaping gazelle. And other times I am scrambling to get up to the top, and the creepers won't let me. I slither down them.'

'How do you feel when you're doing this, trying to climb the creepers?'

'Terrified. There are dogs at my heels.'

'Are you alone?'

Rachel hesitated. 'No. Sometimes my mother's there and she is throwing rocks at the dogs and some run off yelping.' She paused. 'Some come and attack her, drag at her cardigan; the hem of her skirt.'

'What do you do then?'

'Sometimes I scramble even harder to get up the column.' She paused. 'Sometimes it seems I am one of the dogs, tearing and pulling at her, wanting to draw blood.' She threw her hand up in the air. 'How can I dream that? Me? Why?'

Daisy smiled her easy smile. 'That's what we're here for, Miss Waterman. To do some very hard work so that we can, if not find the answers, at least change the kind of questions you are asking. Now ... would it be too much to ask you about your mother? How you see her now, your mother, how you saw her when you were a child ...?'

CHAPTER FIFTEEN

ALEX VAN DORN

Ian helped the old man down the steps into the enclosed courtyard garden; the elbow and the upper arm under his hand seemed to creak like old paper. As always, they talked.

'So your grandmother's visit wasn't a hundred per cent success.' Alex Van Dorn had become lighter and less substantial in the years he had visited Ian. It seemed now as though he would be carried away on the wind.

'You heard?'

'Mr MacIntire said it was something of a tense occasion.'

'Never misses a trick, Mac.'

'It's his job, Ian. We've agreed before, haven't we, that you can't blame a man for doing his job? So how do you see her, your grandmother?'

'I see it like this, Mr V. Maureen Sobell—my Nana—well, she just knows no better. She said when she was here that we'd been everything to each other. Well that's cra—sorry. A load of rubbish. But it was true that we were all each other had. That was true. But she never got within an inch of loving me.'

It was the easiest thing in the world now, to be as open as this to Van Dorn, but it had taken

208

three years of patient visiting to get to that point.

'You see she always worshipped our Sandra. But then, like now, she sees herself as the middle of the world. The very centre. I knew that when I was younger, see? And I knew you could use that to work her, to get at her. Then all those things that happened. She sees it like it was about the world being against her. Almost like it was nothing to do with me.'

They walked by an apple tree which had been trained up the stone wall, its natural growth pinned back to symmetrical efficiency.

'I had a grandmother, Ian. She too was the centre of her own world until it was consumed ... Did you ever love her, Ian, your grandmother?'

They walked the whole length of the courtyard.

'Love? I don't know about that Mr V. She was the only one there, see? We were stuck together. Sometimes she made me laugh. I liked it then. Our Sandra, she came and went. Mostly went.'

'But you loved Sandra?'

Ian waited till they turned another corner. 'She was beautiful, you know? Fluttering around like some butterfly. Thinking about it, she was really young, then, Sandra. She must have been expecting me when she was even younger than I am now. Think of it!' He paused. 'To be honest, I don't think she thought anything about me. Nothing. But as she flitted in and out of the house, I thought she was, like, lovely, Mr V. Lovely hair, lovely hands; and she always smelt so nice, Sandra.' He paused again. 'But for her, Mr V, I was like the air. Invisible. At least Mo saw me enough to clout me.'

'I know about that, Ian, about feeling invisible; as though you don't exist.'

'Do you, Mr V?'

'You can be sure that I do.' The old man started to cough. 'Can we sit on the bench? That's enough walking, I think.'

They sat quietly for a few minutes, then Van Dorn turned towards him. 'What will you do Ian, when you ... go from here?'

'*If* I go.'

'Be sure of it, Ian. You will. Sooner or later. What will you do?'

'I want to do something where I can do the whole thing myself, where I can see the beginning, the middle and the end. The whole thing. Not be part of anybody else's routine. Not be in anybody else's power.'

'Mmm. And about the name, Ian. You know you asked me about the name?'

'Yes?'

'I have thought about it. There is no one else. You may have it if you wish. But Ian. You must honour the name. It is the name of my grandmother, and her grandfather. There, my breath is back. We can walk again.'

210

They set off again on their slow journey.

'Ian? Can I ask you a question.'

'Go on.'

'Do you ever think about the little boys? The ones who . . .'

'Played the game? Yes. It's hard. I think about them standing there on the stones. I dream it. I see my fingers torn and bloody from making the piles . . . But I've told the shrinks a thousand times I can't remember what happened. I must believe what they say but there's nothing in my head about it. They have a name for it, but I think they finally believe me. I offered to pretend to remember but they weren't having any.'

'It could effect your release; you know that?'

Ian nodded. 'But they know I feel remorse, and they know I believe it was me, but I can't . . .' His voice trembled. The old man put a hand on his. He coughed. 'Do you think there are such things as ghosts, Mr V.?'

'I think there are presences over and above the physical . . . Why do you ask?'

'About that time I saw this lad, not Mikey or Jonno; about that time. I think he was from years back. Those shrinks, early days, tried to make out he was telling me to do it. Someone bleated to the papers and there was articles about me listening to the promptings of Satan.'

'And was he, prompting you?'

'Nah. But I think he was like me. He knew it, and wanted to say about himself. But he didn't egg me on. He had done some horrible thing and he was sorry, but I think he wanted me to be sorry for him. To show he was there, in the world. Not some bit of rubbish. Like me!'

'Is this not a dream?'

'Nah. He was as solid as you sitting there. And I'm telling you, he stank like a pig in muck.'

Alex Van Dorn laughed; a chirruping sound which rippled across the courtyard. 'My grandmother in Holland, she was a countrywoman; she always said you would know the old ones, the ones who had gone, with your nose. I think she might say you are like souls calling each other across the centuries. You have not seen him here, or in the other prison? Not since?'

'In dreams, yes. But as a living stinking human being, no. But he's there. That's another thing I'll do, one day: show him that I know that he's sorry and that I'm sorry for him.'

'Do you think it will make up for the others? The two little ones?'

Ian stood up. 'No. Never. Nothing can do that. But I can't begin to even try to understand it until I remember, and when I really try all there is, is this great black hole inside me. It's like shouting across the abyss.' He shivered.

Alex Van Dorn hauled himself to his feet. 'Yes, Ian, it is getting chilly. Shall we go in and find a nice cup of tea?'

PART THREE

HERE AND NOW

There once lived a princess
A princess, a princess
There once lived a princess
A long time ago
Her first name was Snowdrop
Snowdrop, Snowdrop
Her first name was Snowdrop
A long time ago . . .

(For skipping . . .)

CHAPTER SIXTEEN

THE ABYSS

1979

Alex Van Dorn, nee Ian Sobell, was shaking and sweating when he got back from Rachel Waterman's house. The hotel receptionist was very concerned at his grey face, his shaking hands. 'You look like death, sir,' she said.

'Just had a bit of a shock, that's all.'

'Why don't you let Marlene here have the littl'ns for an hour. She can take them down to the kitchens and they can have some ice-cream, or chocolate or something.' She reached across and plucked Sophie from his arms. Charlie was already toddling round to the sacred territory behind the desk. 'Can I have ice-cream?' asked Charlie.

'Not chocolate,' said Ian automatically. 'They're allergic to chocolate.'

'Well sir, don't you worry. Go and get your head down.'

He sat on the hard bed and lowered his head on his hands, allowing the shock to travel through him, now the children were safely in other hands. He could see it now, as clearly as a film on a screen before him. The abyss in full colour. He reached the phone and dialled a number. It took them minutes to find her.

'Maggie, something's happened.'

'What is it, Alex? What is it?' She latched onto his panic; her voice was sharp.

'I went to see the teacher, like I told you...'

'Was she horrible?'

'No. She was all right. But shocked, and she fainted.'

'And?'

He started to shake.

'Alex! For God's sake, what happened?'

'Charlie cried. And ... and...'

'What? What?'

He sighed. 'I remembered, Maggie. I remembered.'

'Stay where you are, lover. I'm coming. I'll be there first thing.'

He lay back on the bed and tried to stop the images flashing before his eyes.

The telephone rang. It was reception. 'Mr Van Dorn? How are you? The children are asking...'

'I'll come down.'

* * *

The next day Alex had to stop the car twice to ask the way, before he found his way to Maureen Godwit's council house. It was part of a mixed estate, some old, some new, being part of a programme of infill-building which had eaten up the fields which lined the roads on

216

the way up to the Old Cross.

'Ian! It's you! And this is your littl'n. Come in.' The words were welcoming, but her manner was guarded. He wasn't there at her invitation. He had written and said he would come to see her.

She closed the sitting room curtains although normally it entertained her to keep her eye on the street these evenings when Reg was at work. She did not relish the idea that other people might be entertained by the sight of her visitor.

She stood uneasily by the window while Ian sat down, pulling the child in beside him.

He looked round the room, his watchful eye noting the neat dralon three piece suite, the big video, the glass coffee table and the wallpaper with alternate stripes of red and blue roses.

'Looks like you're doing all right...' He couldn't use her name. He couldn't call her anything now. Not Mo. Not Maureen. Not Nana.

'Well, Reg's doing all right. Well paid on nightshift. He's there now.'

One of the five letters he had had from her in the last sixteen years had been a note confirming that she had married Reg Godwit and that she had worn bridal white. Ian had sent her a present—a wooden seal that had taken him two weeks to make. It was rather a good one, in applewood that he had buried for two years to allow for slow drying. He had rubbed the surface to a silky smoothness that reflected light like the wet back of a seal. He had been really pleased with it. Maureen hadn't written to say whether it had arrived. He looked more closely at the shelves, into the corners of the neat room. There was no sign of it.

'Would you like a beer?' She pushed a can and a glass into his hand. 'The baby? What'll he have?'

'She'll have some milk,' he said shortly.

'Fine baby. Favours you. Is your wife fair?'

'No. She's dark. Very dark.'

She sat down clutching a tall glass of orange squash, in the easy chair furthest away from him. 'She didn't come with you.'

'No. She had to go away. Something to do with work. So I thought I'd come up here with the children...'

'Children?' she said.

'The toddler, Charlie, is back at the hotel playing on the computer with the receptionist's assistant...' He looked at her through narrowed eyes. 'Does Reg know I'm here?'

'Well, no Ian. He's ... I wasn't sure that you'd actually arrive, so it wasn't worth ... He would have been all right about it, like. I've no beds made up or anything.' She hurried on.

'No need to worry, Mo.' He finally brought her name across his lips. 'I'm booked in at that Swan Hotel, two miles out. Towards the motorway.'

218

This impressed her. 'Pricey, that! You workin' then?'

'I've always worked. When I was inside, I worked and now I'm outside, I work.'

'What's it you do?'

'I have this garage. Selling, repairs, maintenance. Started small, quite big now. More work than I can do with. As well as that I carve these wooden figures. They sell to the galleries and that. One reason why I'm up here. Whole batch of them to Sheffield and to Edinburgh.' He looked round. 'What happened to your carving? The seal?'

She went red. He noticed now how much broader she was—broader in the face, broader in the body. She was wearing a neat half-apron over a crimplene pleated skirt. To all appearances she looked the soul of respectability. He looked her hard in the eye.

'The seal? It was real nice. Life-like. The thing is, Ian, our Sandra took a real fancy to it, so I thought I'd let her have it. Took it back to London one time when she came up.' She paused, then said, 'You have this garage, you said?'

'Yeah. Need to work for yourself, people like me. Degrees and diplomas, but nobody likely to take you on, placed like I am. They'd have to know. Started off with some financial help from that bloke who visited me while I was inside. Man named Van Dorn. Paid him back to the penny last year...'

Alex Van Dorn was very fragile now, living in a sparse ground floor flat in North London. However, he was always sparky on his namesake's twice-yearly visits; interested in his affairs, and making jokes about being the one receiving the visits these days.

'... So how's Sandra now?' He did not want to talk to her about Van Dorn. That would be a kind of pollution.

'All right. Really well I think. But I don't hear from her that often. You know she got divorced, then married to this man, the one with all the flower shops?'

He didn't. He shook his head slowly, staring at her and she became flustered and blurted it all out. 'Well she has this nice house in Tooting, and two little girls.'

Ian followed her gaze to the television, on top of which was a photograph with a heavily modelled frame. In it two girls, aged perhaps seven and eight, were sitting side by side in matching blue velvet tracksuits with yellow bands in their blonde hair.

Maureen blundered on. 'It was a pity about her career, though. She was just getting some good chances when she met him. But he made her give all that up. Wanted her to devote herself to her family...' Her voice faded away.

'Tooting?' he said, pulling a small notebook out of the inner pocket of his jacket. 'Give me her number and I'll give her a bell sometime. I get up to London now and then.'

220

Taking a deep breath, Maureen regained control of herself. 'Well, Ian, it's tucked away somewhere. I might not be able to put my hand on it.'

'You mean you won't give it me?'

'Something like that.' She looked straight at him. There was a faintly triumphant note in her voice; almost playful. In the long silence which followed he stared at her. She was just the same really, despite the sedate house and the comfortable middle-aged spread.

She hurried to change the subject. 'Your voice Ian. It's different...'

'That? That's partly institutions, partly Australia, where I was for five years on licence, when I came out. And part the West Country where I live now.'

'It sounds dead funny.'

He laughed. 'Have you heard yourself lately?'

'There's no need for that,' she flashed.

Feeling the strain, the baby started to whimper and Maureen stood up and leaned towards her, smiling. 'Poor mite...'

He knocked her hands away. 'Leave her alone. Keep your hands off her.' The words rolled out, the Devonshire drawl very strong, the menace in them very clear.

She shrugged, sat down again, and smiled across at him, quite pleased at his anger. 'No need to lose your wool, Ian.'

'I've just been to see Miss Waterman...'

'Her? You want nothing seeing her.'

'She's all right.'

'All right? She's as cracked as a pot. In and out of the loony bin.'

'Not so. Just once, she was in.'

'How would you know that? I always said it was up to her. It was her, Ian; all her fault. All that business. If she hadn't had all you lot up in that filthy old place, none of it would have happened. Not those two kids, not you burning down my house with meself in bed.'

Alex was sitting forward now in the comfortable chair. 'Don't talk rubbish, Mo.' The name was now easier. Put them on equal footing. 'No way it was Miss Waterman's fault. One thing I did learn properly in prison, as well as how to carve wood, was that it was my fault. I did it. It was down to me, see? I was sorry right away, even if I was ready for the loony bin myself. If you're keen to lay fault you might say that it was your fault, or that it was Sandra's. But no way was it Miss Waterman's.'

She was up now, and shouting, much more her old self. 'Well that's where you're wrong, clever dick with your hayseed talk. It was her fault. She knew it; I knew it. She said so.'

'Said so?'

'It was that time, when she went to the loony bin ... I told you, didn't I? A few years after that business over you. I got myself upset again.'

Alex recognised from other days Maureen's

euphemism for 'fighting drunk'.

'There was another piece in the paper about Satan's children. Our Sandra had gone down London and people were still looking at me behind their hands. I was out of that burned-down house and into another place by then.'

'So?'

'So I went there to see her; to tell her.' She smiled. 'I gave her a bloody good hiding. I can tell you. Knew it was her fault. Even then she said it was her fault; agreed with me. She said it. Shouted it. Shouting away, screaming away.'

'So what happened. The police . . .?'

'Well, they mebbe would have got the police, bloody snobs, but the mother started ranting and raving, then collapsed. It was ambulances not the police. The old girl to the hospital and her snobbish majesty off to the loony bin.'

'How do you know that?'

'It was all the talk the next day. In a place like this everything gets round.'

'Nothing happened to you at all?'

'Nah. I just crept off. She mustn't 'a said anything, loony as she was.' Maureen smiled faintly.

Alex stood up, pulling the baby onto his hip. 'Well, Mo. I'm off.'

She had had time to think about the garage, to take in his affluent air. 'Come again, Ian. Bring your wife . . .'

'No,' he interrupted her coolly. 'I won't come again. I'd be ashamed to bring her here to talk to you, or get to know your tart of a daughter.'

'What? What? Ashamed? Get out! Get out, you bloody murdering bastard! Get out! Wait till I tell Reg about you. He'll give you a bloody good hiding. You were always short of that...'

He could hear her screams as he strapped the baby in the back of the car, and revved the engine very loud to cut out the noise of her voice in his head as he roared away.

*　　　*　　　*

Rachel sat up, staring into total blackness. She opened her eyes wide, wide, wider to encompass any fragments of light that there might be in the corners of space. There were none. The blackness began to move in on her, to seep into her, to blot up the fragments of light even inside herself. She opened her mouth to shout, to call from the depths of her body. At first there was no sound, but at last— 'Mothe-e-r!'

The darkness receded; the spell was broken. The room was dappled with light and shade; the light from the streetlamp filtering through the curtains. She breathed slowly in the way she had learned in the hospital, and the room threatened her no longer.

When she saw the figure in the corner, one part of her mind told her she was in the familiar dream-state.

224

It was the boy from the path. He moved forward. 'You all right, Missis?' His light echoey voice showed concern. His hands hung down in front of him, loose and ungainly.

'Yes. I am all right.' She pulled her duvet up to her chest. 'What is it you want?'

'I just wanted to tell, to tell yeh. I just knew yeh were t'one I could tell.'

Talking like this, her dream mind told her, he must come from right up the valley. It was a strong accent.

'What's your name?' she said, the echo of teacherly briskness in her voice.

'Philip. Philip Wales. Pip, they say, like.'

'And what will you tell me? And why me?'

'I seen you walking around. I knew you would listen about it. Like the lad, you'd listen about it.'

'About what?'

'About the game. The game we played. The game they made me play.'

'What game?'

'The game on the farm. They made me play the game, then they...' The voice faded, although the mouth was still moving.

She shook her head hard. 'Speak up,' she shouted across a broad abyss, across the space to the moon. She blinked her eyes; he was getting harder and harder to see. 'Stay. Don't go!' Tears were falling down her face, blinding her to his image altogether.

The light clicked; the room was lit from the

centre; the boy was gone. Elena was at the door.

'Rache! Are you all right?'

Rachel dabbed at her face with the corner of the duvet and settled down in the bed. 'I'm fine,' she said calmly. 'Dreaming again, I think.'

'You were shouting.'

'It was a very loud dream.'

'Rache?'

But Rachel was fast asleep again.

Four hours later, Rachel was still heavily asleep when Elena elbowed her way noisily into the bedroom carrying a breakfast tray.

'Here you are.'

'You shouldn't.'

'You just make the most of me when I'm up here. Doesn't happen too often.' The tray held cereal, toast, a pot of coffee, and a paper flower in a specimen vase. 'I've tucked a note in, there beside the coffee jug. I rang that Daisy Montague woman. She said she'd meet you for tea in the Buttery at the Courthouse Hotel. Four o'clock sharp.'

'Elena!'

'It's fixed!'

She pulled at Rachel's pillow with an expert hand. The doorbell rang. 'There's my taxi. Look. I'll phone you when I get there. Are you sure you're all right?'

'Stop mothering me, Ellie!'

'OK. I'm off.' She paused.

226

'Ellie, will you get yourself away?'

She threw the paper flower, and Elena caught it neatly. She grinned and tucked it into the clasp of her bag.

'Bye then!'

'Bye!'

Rachel got down to the business of buttering her toast. By the time she had spread it to the furthest corners of the slice she heard the door bang downstairs, followed by the roar of the taxi. She was finally on her own again. Despite everything, it was a good feeling.

CHAPTER SEVENTEEN

THE TUMBRIL

'Funny place for a consultation,' said Daisy Montague, leaning across to pour some more tea from the battered silver teapot.

Rachel's gaze drifted past the other woman to the self-conscious authenticity of the wallpaper and artful prints of the Courthouse Hotel at various points in its long history. People had been fed and watered in this old building for more than six hundred years. For one period in its history they were tried and sentenced there as well; the 'Courthouse' name had stuck. But there was no taste, no flavour of other times in the air; a flavour she could taste in many other old buildings. It was as though all the improvements, the glamorous authentication, had blotted up every stain, every trace, every breath of the real people who had walked in these rooms through time.

'Miss Waterman ... Rachel?'

Daisy Montague's high voice and blinding smile pierced into her wandering mind like a knife through gauze.

Her gaze fixed back onto the woman's small neat face. 'I'm sorry Mrs Montague. Miles away. Is your teacake all right?'

Daisy Montague took her knife and spread butter on a second piece of teacake. She had aged in the ten years since Rachel had first seen her. Her round eyes looked blandly across, through round National Health spectacles. Rachel wondered, in an abstracted fashion, about this. Surely a consultant psychiatrist with a national reputation could run to decent glasses?

'You're going away from me again, Miss Waterman! You used to do that all the time.'

'Am I? Sorry about that. You're right. It is a funny place for a consultation. I couldn't have come up to your rooms again, but really Elena is very naughty to have...'

'Your sister is overwhelmingly persuasive. She is a very good nurse, I believe. Her reputation goes before her. She thought it would be too much of a reminder for you. It was a hard time for you. And others.'

228

'You're right there, I've had enough of the hospital to last me a lifetime. Pills. Machines. Long, long talks. It helped, but when I came out I decided never to go there again. I won't even go past it in the bus. Take any route rather than see it again.' She took up her own butter knife. 'But it was something you said about the murderer that was in all of us that finally clicked with me. I've been thinking about that lately. So it's good of you to come here...'

'It is, rather, isn't it?' Daisy Montague's even white teeth bit into the yielding teacake. 'Against the rules, really.' There was a pause. 'Did it bother you, her going away; living away? Your sister?'

'That? No! I wanted her out from under for years. I should have gone myself at her age.'

The other woman stayed silent.

'Oh, you're thinking I'm protesting too much? That I really am bothered? It's not like that. Truly. She would have found all sorts of excuses to stay. It could be quite irritating.'

Daisy disposed of a crumb at the corner of her mouth with a dainty finger. 'But there are things troubling you just now, aren't there Rachel? May I call you Rachel?'

Here we go, she thought, the 'I-am-the-mother.' 'Only if I can call you Daisy.'

The other woman hesitated, the pink of her apple cheeks deepening. 'If the alternative is for me to call you Miss Waterman, you may call me Daisy.'

Rachel grinned suddenly. 'Against your better judgement?'

'Is it? Well this whole thing is unorthodox anyway. That sister of yours ... Well now, what about these things, these feelings ...?'

'They are not feelings. They are facts. Things that have really happened to me.'

'What things?'

'I have seen two people—boys.'

'They make you think about what happened years ago.'

'You know about that, of course. My notes. And my helpful and persuasive sister!'

'She said you had a look in your eye that you had then. I think you frightened her a bit. Even the formidable nurse.' Daisy leaned over to pour more tea into the two china cups.

'Well, anyway. It's not just feelings. One of these two boys has the name ... the name of a boy from then. *The* boy ... But now he's a man. A complete stranger. He came, and I got myself upset, and I started to black out again. Just like before; the other times.

'Then there is this other one. He *is* just a boy. Comes and goes like a will-o'-the-wisp. In the pathway; in the garden. Even in the corner of my bedroom. And I think I saw him before, much earlier, but I can't remember where. Now that one is odd. A kind of extended dream. But he is solid. I felt him bump me. But the other one is not a dream, the man who was the boy. He sat there with his baby and his little boy and drank coffee. And then somehow, these boys, they are both the same.'

'You see them both as real people?'

'Well the one who drank the coffee certainly is. The other one, I don't know. But he *seems* so real. I *felt* the bump as he ran past me on the footpath. He felt as physical as this table.'

'How do you feel now, Rachel? No panic? Not faint?'

'No. Right as rain.'

'You cope all right in the house on your own?'

'I like it. Elena's gone back again now, and I'm relieved.' She curled a fist, large for a woman, on the white tablecloth.

She sat quite tall. Her hair was thick and long, pulled back in a rather dated fashion. She was wearing a jumper over her cotton shirt, fastened with a neat gold brooch at the neck. Neat. Self-contained. No wild thing. But, thought Daisy ruefully, she had seemed calm enough, those years before. Between the screaming panics, the explosions of guilt, and the recriminations.

'Look, let's get another pot of tea,' said Daisy, having made her decision, 'and you can tell me more. So I can get a fuller picture. That might be a help.'

Rachel stood up, grasping her leather shoulder-bag. 'No. I don't think so. I don't want ... need to think about it now, even less tell about it.'

'Something's making you think about it.'

'I know.' She shrugged herself into a big wool coat and was gone, leaving Daisy to pay the bill.

Daisy ran after her, puffing for breath. They stood on the pavement outside the Buttery, just looking at each other. Rain which was not quite rain, solidified from the air and clung to their coats, hanging there like dew-drops.

Daisy peered up at Rachel with that soft mixture of feather and claw that makes up an owl. 'I need to see you again. You need me to see you again. At home? Sunday at five?'

Rachel looked down at her, distracted again. 'If you want,' she said vaguely.

'In that case, I'll see you then.'

Then Rachel was watching her bustling little figure as she whirled back into the Courthouse Buttery to pay for their teas.

*   *   *

Rachel's journey home on the bus took a good twenty minutes. During that time there was never more than four other people on the bus as it stopped and started, picking up and dropping off its passengers.

She watched the familiar scenes pass the window, half-mesmerised by the lurching sway of the bus. This was a route as old as the history of the county, well documented in the history books.

Rachel always knew when she was on an old road, even when its age was not public knowledge. Even without checking she would know, in her bones, that a road was old. She sometimes saw other travellers too, half-closing her eyes and looking inward as well as outward. She would see carriages and carts bumping and swaying, mud dropping off the rims of high wheels as they turned. She would see heavy horses, sometimes with three people aboard, like so many sprawling sacks of potatoes.

She had seen some travellers on this same long route sixteen years before, travelling by coach back to Oak Ridge; on the day of the hearings, the day of the interminable questions. From her place on the bus she had seen not just a cart, but crowds of people shouting and whistling, even throwing stones. She had actually ducked to dodge one of these missiles, and a woman on the bus beside her had swung round, glaring at her.

Then she had screwed her eyes tighter, only allowing in the barest lick of light to clarify the image. She saw soldiers or militia-men on the cart. One of them was holding onto a small figure which was tethered from behind. A small figure; no more than a child. No less a child than Ian Sobell who had been the subject of the intense and prolonged questioning she had just endured.

Then the image had vanished and she had

started to cry. The woman who had been so outraged before put her arms round her and comforted her.

Now, on this journey, thinking about her recent meeting with Daisy Montague, she tried to do the trick again, concentrating hard, screwing up her eyes to make the old road appear. Two motorbikes passed the bus at speed and the bus driver yelled at them, pipping his horn. The scene was so contemporary that she smiled briefly and abandoned her attempt at recall.

As she alighted very carefully from the bus, she had the sudden and total thought that it was time she had a car again. Yes, it really was time she bought a car. Getting away from Oak Ridge could start with short journeys.

Walking slowly along the path by the hedge she looked around keenly, even eagerly, for the boy, but there was no sign of him.

Once inside she left her coat on and made a mug of coffee. Instead of settling down with it in front of the gas fire, she went outside, up into the garden. She pulled an old canvas folding-chair up into the high part at the back of the lawn and sat down in the soft evening light. Her peace was only marginally disturbed by the distant pulsing gear-change of heavy vehicles as they roared away from the Old Cross.

The coffee was good. She opened the book on her lap and began to turn the pages.

'I need to talk to you, Missis.'

With the side of her eyes, then, turning her head, with the whole of her eyes, she saw the boy. He was leaning against the broad trunk of the old tree that marked the top of the garden.

The boy was not agitated, as he had been out in the dark; not tense as he had seemed in the bedroom. He was quite calm, his dark face looking straight at her. She took a deep breath and relaxed. Dream or life, he was no threat. She knew children.

'I come here because this is where you are. Mostly I'm at the crossroads, or the Three Spike. Here's as far as I can get away. And then, not always. Can't get away, see?'

'Three Spike? Where's that?'

'Down there.' His hand waved in the general direction of the town. 'By the river.'

She had a sudden vision of the Old Baths. That's where he was talking about. Of course the baths would be by the river.

She felt so comfortable, so tranquil that she only just drew back from offering him biscuits. And a bath, she thought, wrinkling her nose just a bit. It was like Siskin in that first year.

She leaned forward. 'I want you to tell me,' she said urgently. 'Pip! Did you say it was Pip? It happened to you and to Ian. Is that what you're telling me? I want you to tell me.'

Then she could see through him to the shrub behind and a moment later he was gone.

CHAPTER EIGHTEEN

THE HOUSE IN TENWORTH GARDENS

There was no answer the first time Rachel rang, so she put down the phone and dialled the number again. She thought of the years that had raced past since they had last spoken. He wasn't dead; she knew that. In a place as small as Oak Ridge that would have been news. It would have been in the paper as had the death of Keith Warner:

'An esteemed teacher and headteacher of this town has died, after a long illness, bravely born.'

This second time, the phone was picked up before the third ring.

'Yes?' The voice was smoky, cross and creaky with age, but very familiar.

'Jack, this is Rachel Waterman . . .'

'Is it, begad! Rachel! Well dearie, this is a surprise. Thought you'd chucked me aside, along with your passion for the great game of cricket. Years ago. Well, dearie, how are you?'

'Well, Jack, really well!'

'And how's the lovely sister?'

'Smashing. She's working in London now, Jack. Just gone back. Promotion, and a bigger hospital.'

'Married, I bet.'

'No. There is a man. But I don't know. She's not that keen.'

'Young people seem less and less keen today. Not wanting to be tied down. Good thing, I suppose.'

'How about you, Jack. How are you?'

'Well, not married again, if that's what you mean. Once bitten, seventeen times shy. As for the rest, you might say I'm not a hundred per cent. Legs are bad; some kind of arthritis. Have to resort to the dreaded wheelchair outside...' His voice went thin there and she thought of the lively roar with which he had made generations of children sit up straight.

'Jack, you should have let me know.'

'No point, was there? Anyway, dearie, you sound right perky yourself. What can I do for you? I'm sure you're not just calling for calling's sake.'

'Well, yes,' she hesitated. She promised herself faithfully that she'd go to visit him the minute this business was sorted. 'I do want to check on something. I thought you were the one to help. Do you remember Ian Sobell?'

There was a silence, then a rustle as he moved his telephone to the other hand. 'Do I? Yes of course I do, you know that ... Dearie, you're not going to get yourself all upset again are you?'

'No. That's behind me, it really is. It's just that I want to trace the woman. The grandmother. Maureen, was it?'

Jack knew the Siskin community. He always knew the name, pedigree and approximate whereabouts of the generations of children he had barked at and marshalled through the years at the school.

'But she came and belted ... Why do you want to know?'

She hesitated. 'Well ... Ian: he came round...'

'Wha—at?'

'He's been out some time apparently. Anyway, he called round. Really amiable, he was. So changed—but aren't they all after that time? Anyway, like a fool, I passed out. And I really wanted to see him. Talk to him properly.'

'Want to?'

'Yes. Need to.'

There was a long silence.

'Well,' he said finally, with some reluctance, 'They pulled down The Squares, where she moved after the lad burned her house. All that network was demolished. Good riddance to bad Sixties rubbish I say. New superstore now. You'd know that?'

'Yes. I know that.'

'The families were rehoused. Up in those new flats at Forest Row.'

'So she's somewhere there?'

'Well, no.' He paused.

'Where is she, Jack?'

'She's out at Tenworth Gardens. The council estate. Better end. Gone all respectable now. Comely enough woman. She was no age to be a grandma, now was she? Does cricket teas, dare I say? She married Reg Godwit. Good feller. Captain of the second team. Trains the youngsters. Good allrounder. His wife left him for the second best batsman of the first team. Hell of a hitter *he* was. She took her three children with her. Teenagers. Went off to Doncaster. Not sure whether he still plays, down in Doncaster. Suppose he will, Yorkshire being what it is.'

'Jack! If this Reg Godwit's a cricketer you'll know exactly where he lives. How many years were you club secretary?'

'Look, dearie. Let me come with you ...'

'No.' she said firmly. 'What number?'

'Right! It was his mother's house. One-two-four Tenworth Gardens. That's it. Like you say, I've got them all off by heart. Even get down to the club in me wheelchair most nights. Good chat in the bar. They're very good down there.'

'Well, anyway, thanks Jack. You come up trumps every time.'

'Except that time I tried to push an old man's luck?'

She could feel the hearty grin come down the lines of the telephone. It had been a half-hearted attempt, but had stopped her going to cricket matches. 'Except that time!'

'Anyway, just come down and see an old feller some time. Won't you?'

'I'll do that.' But now she knew she wouldn't.

*   *   *

The garden of the house in Tenworth Gardens was neat to the point of extinction. There were neat squares of cast concrete at the centre, where grass grew in the other gardens. The narrow border was marked by a rosebush at intervals of precisely two feet. Each rosebush had been pruned back severely for the winter. Each corner of the garden was graced by a clump of anonymous herbaceous plants. Nothing in the garden was taller than eighteen inches high.

Rachel pushed hard at the bell and stood listening to the whispered echo of Brahms' lullaby as it whirred through the house.

The door was opened by a man with a bald head, round as a baby's and a moustache as neatly pruned as his rosebushes. His short-sleeved sports shirt showed off his muscular arms to advantage. He looked at her in easy enquiry.

'I've come to see Maureen Sobell—Godwit...' She said politely. 'Is she in?'

He opened the door another foot and nodded, then turned in the small hall to put his head round the sitting room door. 'Mo! Somebody for you!' Then he vanished back into the kitchen.

240

                    *   *   *

Maureen was tucking the *Evening Chronicle* into a neat square as she came to the door. She looked up at Rachel blankly; her face cleared, then clouded over again. 'What is it?' she said, keeping her voice quite neutral.

Rachel looked along the street in both directions. 'Could I come in a second, Mrs— Godwit, is it?'

Her tone, her demeanour, were humble enough.

'Well, all right,' said Maureen, leading her through the sitting room door. One part of her mind took in her own nice room with its own nice things. Things had changed now. Who would be high and mighty with her now? Who could come and tell her to collect prescriptions, and the like?

She didn't ask Rachel to sit, but turned to face her across the smoked glass coffee table. She smiled with thin courtesy, touching her neat short hair. 'What can I do for you?'

'Ian. He came to my house.'

'Yeah. He came here too.' She held her silence.

'Well. He went off too quickly. I didn't really have a chance to talk to him. I need to talk to him.'

Maureen turned round towards the teak mantelshelf, picked up a packet and lit a cigarette. Rachel watched through the mirror as the older woman lifted her clear grey eyes and looked into hers. 'Like I say, he came here as well. He's in some lousy mood. Did he ... was he ... did he say anything to you?'

'No. No. He was very nice. Polite. There was a little boy and a baby with him. He just went off very quickly.'

'He's changed.' Maureen pointed to a seat with the hand that still held the cigarettes and the matches.

Rachel sat down obediently.

'He was such a nice kid before all that business. Do anything for me, he would. I never believed it when they said he fired the house knowing I was in it. Didn't know him like I did.'

Rachel stayed silent.

'He must have made something of hisself since he came out. Did you see the car?'

'No.'

'But he was mean when he came. Real mean. Never been before. Not since ... And when he comes, he's that mean. He wasn't like he was before. Those places! Ruin them, they do!'

'I thought he looked—well—fine. The baby and the little boy looked ... well. It's just that I wanted a few more words with him,' she persisted.

'Like I say, though. He's changed, now. Vicious,' said Maureen, ignoring her.

Rachel looked blankly at her, wondering at the other woman's ability to skirt around the terrible truth of the dead boys. She talked as though it were all about her and the fire.

Maureen placed her lips to the long golden tip of the cigarette and drew on it. Then she looked straight at Rachel. 'Your mother. I saw in the paper she ... passed on.'

'It was a heart attack. She often got carried away with things. All kinds of things. It could have happened any time.'

Maureen looked at the tip of her cigarette then across again at Rachel. 'I know, like, that you could have laid us in for that thing I did. I get stupid when I get a bit upset. Always did. Them round here would have loved it, me in trouble as well as Ian. Me up in court after that other business. Hard enough to live with it anyway.'

'I was in hospital myself awhile then ... I'm a bit stupid myself, when I get worked up ... I really do need to talk to Ian, Mrs Godwit...'

'Well ... I don't really know where he actually lives. Hasn't bothered to keep in touch. In spite of the fact he's done so well. Exams, degrees, inside. Did you know he got them?'

'Not really. I knew he had a good brain. I'm pleased he managed to use it.'

'The things they do for them inside now! It's a holiday camp. But anyway, he did say he's staying at the Swan Hotel; that's on the road coming into Oak Ridge.'

Rachel stood up. 'Thank you Mrs Godwit.

I'm sorry to disturb you. I know how hard it is.'

'That's all right,' said Maureen magnanimously. 'You watch yourself with him, mind. He has this bad streak in him. Like all them boys. Give me girls any day. It's a sister you have, isn't it?'

'Yes.'

'And both doing well? Your mother was a lucky woman. Give me girls any time. You know where you are with girls...'

Rachel ran the length of the street and then leaned against the wall to retrieve her breath, and to stop the waves of nausea that seemed to be flooding from her feet to her throat. The cost of finding Ian's whereabouts had been high. Still she knew now, where to find him.

* * *

'Alex Van Dorn.' The voice was distant, authoritative.

'Alex ... Ian ... This is Rachel Waterman. I need to come and talk to you. I must have passed out when you came to see me. Foolish of me.'

His tone changed entirely. 'Miss Waterman? I'm sorry about that. It was a naff trick, seeing you with no warning. Stupid kind of test, I suppose.'

'You're not unique, you know. You'd be surprised how many people try it on with their old teachers. People I've taught years before,

244

teasing me with who they really are...'

'Sorry about rushing off as well. The baby cried and I panicked. You seemed basically all right, so I thought I'd best go. I was a bit spooked myself, thinking about the last time I was at the house.'

'Anyway. My sister came. Fell over me in the dark, actually. I still want to talk with you, Ian—Alex...'

'Me too. To tell you ... I was just packing up to go. I'm going back south tomorrow. But we could talk before that...' A baby's wail bloomed out of the background and she could hear him making soothing noises. 'I have a present for you, and I've found something I want to show you.'

'A present?' She was uneasy.

'Don't worry. It's nothing very much. I made it myself; finished it not very long ago. It was when I made it I knew I needed to come and see you.'

'It sounds mysterious.'

'Not really. But it is in a way. Can I come and collect you in the morning? Seven o'clock?'

She was silent for a moment. The risks. Her mother would have said the newspapers were full of dead women who took such risks.

'Is that too early? It's just that I have to be in Worcester by twelve to pick up my wife. She's at college there, on a course.'

'No. No. Seven o'clock is quite all right. Absolutely. Your wife—she's a student?'

245

'No. It's a short course on marketing. As well as the garage, we make things, and she sells them. I'll tell you tomorrow. So I can collect you?'

'Where are we going?'

'Well, it's something I've found out while I've been here. You'll see.'

The phone went dead and she gazed at the handset. Locating her particular feeling, she recognised it as that combination of intrigue, excitement and the fear she had felt the few times she had arranged a date with a man in her youth. She almost looked over her shoulder for the over-eager eyes of her mother, curious in a hungry fashion about her daughter's youthful assignations.

Rachel poured herself a gin with a long splash of tonic and went across to stare out of the window into the long back garden where she had last seen the boy. She loosened her mind out, and closed her eyes to a squint, but there was no sign, no feeling of him.

It seemed a long time since Elena had left. A very long time.

CHAPTER NINETEEN

IAN TELLS HIS TALE

'No little ones today?' Rachel slid into the passenger seat, peering at the child's harness, empty in the back.

'Maggie's here. That's my wife. Got a lift from someone coming up this way. I rang her and she came straight off. Anyway, it was very late so I didn't want to disturb you with another call. Maggie wanted to set off first thing, but I said I needed the morning for this unfinished business.' He put the car smoothly into gear. His voice still reflected the West Country; softer than normal around here, broadening into a drawl.

'Unfinished business?' She was conscious of begging the question in more than one way.

'You know. I think you know. Something happened to me that night in your house, when you fainted and the baby started to cry. I remembered something that has been a blank to me for a lot of years.'

She was still a little uneasy. 'Where're we going Ian?'

'You'll soon see.'

The car moved smoothly through the familiar streets. She noted the darkness of the morning, registering mild surprise as she saw the steady stream of cars, the bus stops full of people. The factory, that was it. All these people up and about, at their desks and benches by seven-thirty. She remembered a conversation with some friend of Elena's, who worked in the factory offices. Rachel had blanched at the thought of such early hours and listened with some disbelief as he told her that the convenors had consulted the workers on the pattern of a negotiated reduction of hours. The majority of them had voted to make the afternoon shorter, rather than vote for a later start. 'More time for the kids, see? In the afternoons. Wife can do the shopping.'

Now Rachel sat quietly, working on her own composure, as they purred past the factory, with its sentinel gates, its genteel park-planted entrance, its extended ant-eyed walls.

Another two miles and they were in a village that Rachel knew well. The social focus of the village was a rather substantial Free House, famous for its real ale. She had, on occasion, survived the rather rigged-up jollity of a bar-meal there, with Elena and her nursing friends.

The through-road bisected the village green, and was punctuated by the white-painted bus stop, whose windows, every one, were smashed by some vandal's terminal precision.

Alex pulled the car to a neat stop at the iron-gated entrance to the old church, its high tower once a watchguard against cunning and vengeful Scots.

The morning was still threaded with the smoky entrails of the night; the sunrise holding onto the skirts of grey clouds which were building up for a wet September day. Rachel looked with sustained uncertainty at the fair young stranger at her side.

She could feel him take a deep breath as he turned to face her. 'The other day when you fainted and Charlie cried, something happened to me. I always knew I'd done those things to Mikey and Jonno. They told me time and time again and I believed them. But nowhere in my head could I find anything that confirmed what I'd done. I was not allowing myself to know. They talked about defence mechanisms, the shrinks, and thought they could break them down, but they couldn't.

'Then, when you fainted, and Charlie cried in your house, I could hear Mikey's cry again, like he cried that day. Then I could find it all in my head. Oh yes. Then it all rushed into my head, buzzing and charging like colours in a kaleidoscope. I was so spooked I had to get on the phone and tell Maggie to come. I was frightened for myself and the kids. When you rang last night she said I should come and tell you ... talk to you.'

'Ian, please ...'

'If this is too much I'll ...'

'Go on, Ian. What do you want to tell me?'

Two young men, their faces still gummed-up with sleep, raced past the car to leap onto the bus, already moving away from the bus stop.

'Well, I want to tell you what happened that time. Mebba you think you know...' Saying this, his voice seemed to leave behind the West Country drawl; become harder, more like the voice of his childhood. '... But I want to say it to you. Then I want to show you something, that I've found while I've been hanging around plucking up courage to come and see you again. And, as I said on the 'phone, I've got a present for you. Started it ages ago, but only really worked on it and finished it the other week. I brought it for you the other day, but didn't get the chance...'

Now his voice was rougher-edged, easier to recognise. She felt more comfortable, with him speaking in that voice; the voice of the Ian Sobell she remembered, rather than the Alex Van Dorn he was not.

'Well,' she said, with a teacher's asperity in her voice. 'Why not make a start? Tell me what happened. I never really knew; by the time the papers had chewed it up and spat it out it wasn't the action of any human being I knew. Let's get on with it!'

He sat breathing heavily. 'How did the day start? I did always remember that I put the clothes on that morning—the clothes you'd given me. You know—to go to the doctor's?' He had his hands tight on the steering wheel and he was staring straight ahead, through the churchyard gates at the tall unkempt grass that nearly hid the graves. 'I'd spent hours making the game that week and it was really good. The islands were high, well made up. The spaces were right, just right. I was just so excited about the game. The other kids were little, but they'd got the hang of it now. So they could play properly. I had shown them. The game was the best thing that had happened to me in a long time.'

Another long pause. 'So what are you thinking of now? You're in your house...' said Rachel cautiously.

Ian crossed his hands on the steering wheel and put his face on them. At first his voice was muffled. 'I have to wash my face carefully on this morning. I'm looking forward to the day. It is pink soap. A scrap that Sandra's left behind. There's so little trace of her in the house now; she's carried off the whole of herself away in suitcases and carriers. There's just this pink soap, and a lingering perfume that drifts through the door of her bedroom. That's all. I think to myself I'll ask my Nana if I can have Sandra's bedroom. No reason why not.

'I go through to the fireside cupboard in the living room and peer at the blue jumper and the paler blue socks, the ones you gave me. Neatly folded, just as Nana had left them. I pull them out and put the jumper on. The jumper's so soft as it slithers down over my nose, making me sneeze.

'I look at the clock. Ten minutes to three. Just right. I'll get away before Nana gets back from seeing Mrs Armitage.

'Mikey and Jonno are already there at the Old Baths. Jonno's red hair's sticking up at the back, un-combed. Michael has milky tides of food around his mouth. And you know that stuff called sleepy sand in his eyes?

'"See, Ian, didn't I tell you I could tell the time?" says Jonno. He grins, showing his crooked front teeth.

'"Yeah," I says, "Looks like you can, don't it?"

'"It's different here, now." Jonno's looking around the space at my carefully constructed islands, and I'm really pleased. "More places to jump," he says.

'"I put some work in, that's all. Don't say I do nothing for you," I say, using one of my Nana's favourite phrases.

'I stand there real cool, watching the two of them walking aroung the stacks. I know I am smiling at them, pleased with them, and the afternoon, and the clean soft clothes that are flapping against my skin in the afternoon breeze.

'I pull out the giant chocolate bar I bought with some money I took from my Nana's purse. Mikey and Jonno start to grab at it. I hold it high, out of their reach. 'Hang on. Let's get sat down,' I say, boss of it all.

'We sit down on a wall and I share it out into three equal pieces. Mikey eats all of his in hungry gulps; Jonno eats half of his, then puts the rest into his pocket. I sit watching them, enjoying it all. I don't eat my chocolate, I'm too excited to be hungry.

'Then we play the game. It's easier this time. Mikey and Jonno know the rules and join in with buzzing confidence. This time, I relax; I don't chase too hard and I let them catch me now and then.

'One time I'm standing on one of my carefully built high points, watching Mikey desperately chase after Jonno. My foot is stinging a bit with the infection, so I hold it off the ground to relieve it a bit. Something makes me look back at the gate. Through the bars,— dense black stripes in the brightness of the afternoon sun—I can see a round face with a shock of fair hair above it. I look away. My arms and legs are freezing and I start to shake. I'm looking back now and the round face is gone.

'"Come on Ian," Jonno shouts. "You're too long standing. You said you couldn't do that. Against the rules."

'I race around now, playing the game harder to warm my arms and legs. All three of us are shouting and screaming as, in turn, we're caught and make our catches.

'Now I start whistling, loud shrieking whistles, two fingers pressed to the corners of my mouth like I seen Tadger Smith do...

'Jonno is at the top of the highest pile; he

253

spins round when he hears my highest whistle. God, he's losing his footing ... tumbling from the top to the bottom of the pile, the stones are crashing down, crashing down. One larger stone has crashed down before him and his head crashes onto it. He lies very still.

'Running, running to where he is. The blood's trickling, pouring down his face, dripping, covering the chocolate stains. Mikey's screaming now, this high, piping scream like a baby. Oh God people will come ... my Nana'll kill us ... people will come, through the gate, up from the farm. There'll be the cage and the chains ... Cage and chains ...'

Ian was sobbing onto his hands now. Rachel put a hand on his arm; he shook it off.

'"Shut up, Mikey, shut up. Shut up!" My hands're on his mouth, his throat. His teeth sink in my hand. Small teeth as sharp as pincers. Stop it Mikey, stop it. My head hurts, my head hurts. My foot is aching. I throw Mikey hard on the ground. My jumper! My blue jumper! Take it off. Press it on that screaming mouth till the scream becomes a whimper. Keep it there hard till Mikey stops struggling. Take it off now and he's quiet, staring at me with wide eyes, not seeing me; not seeing me ...

'"*Now, shut it, charver!*"' Ian's voice changed for a second, becoming deep and guttural.

Then he went on in his own voice. 'I shake

254

out the sweater and fold it like a pillow and push it under Jonno's head. There Jonno, now you'll be more comfortable. Oh dear, the blood's seeping onto the nice soft blue. Seeping...

'A lot to do! These stones to move; things to arrange. So hot. My hands are sticky. I can't see for sweat in my eyes.

'Now! Who's that at the gate?

'There's a heavy rattle on the bars of the gate and a voice is shouting through. "Let me in! Let me in. Ian! Ian Sobell!! Let us in!"

'I go cold again, icy. I stand up away from the great pile of stones and turn round slowly, towards the face peering through the bars.

'Oh. No problem. It's only Jimmy Denton looking for his little brothers.

'"Now, Jimmy," I say. "They were here, but they're gone now. A policeman is after them. You too. I wouldn't go home if I were you. Don't worry Jimmy; don't worry. Just keep right out of the way and it'll be all right. It'll be all right..." Don't worry Ian, don't worry, Ian. It'll be all right. It'll be all right. Don't worry Ian...' He was sobbing in earnest now, his shoulders heaving.

Rachel put an arm round him and drew him to her, rocking him backwards and forwards. 'Shsh, Ian, shsh, at least now you know. Shsh, shsh. Now you know and you can put it in its place. Shsh, shsh.' She kissed his brow and his hard cheek and her own tears fell onto his white blond hair and mingled with his on his cheek.

CHAPTER TWENTY

LAID TO REST

Rachel's eye caught what she thought was the shadowy figure of a priest in a flapping cloak. She sat up and blinked, to discover in closer perspective it was a crow flopping around from gravestone to gravestone.

Alex sat up straight, took out a pale blue silk handkerchief and blew his nose. 'I never saw all that before. I never knew.'

'Now you do?'

'The other facts. The facts around it; the centre of that day, I've been through a thousand times, especially early on. Police. Shrinks. I was in a state of terror for two years. I felt as though I were truly the Devil. They would try to make me work through it and make me say all that washing and putting on the clothes was some kind of big preparation. You know, some kind of ritual. It might have been; I don't know.'

'But you were only a child. Young even for your years.' She was still fumbling to some kind of understanding.

'It was just ... the game was good, and the

clothes you gave me were so nice. They smelled so nice. Those men seemed always to want me to say it was some kind of ritual preparation; more than just feeling good. As I got my sense of who I was back, through the years, I could never see that. But then I'd say to myself maybe they were right, though. I could never reach far enough into myself to know my real intentions. There were no words then in my head to tell me what I was doing and why. Still, the more I think, the more I think that it was like, you know, when footballers or runners put on their kit in a certain order, and then they know they'll play well.

'I was looking forward to it, the game with Mikey and Jonno. It was a game; a game where the markers were out and the players were designated. But the game wasn't death, Miss Waterman.

'I've thought about those clothes, and worried what you'd think. It wasn't the clothes and it wasn't anything you did, that led to … the thing that happened. I dreamed of you sometimes; a dream where I kept telling you all that, but you drifted away, not hearing …

'Those men talked to me such a lot in the early years. Sometimes for my own good, I know that. Sometimes, I don't know, I think there was an interest in seeing into the mind of a child-killer. Clinical experience, maybe. That might be unfair. I was called pathological, did you know? Behind my back, but I knew that.

Sometimes they would treat me like an ordinary child and act as if I were deaf, or invisible. They let a lot out, those times.

'Anyway, there was one particular fellow who took me through the event, and earlier times in my life too. Through what we did that week, and what had happened in my life ever since I could remember. That was a bit of use. Helped me see a kind of pattern. I still see him now and again. You can never wipe anything out; unmake it. You can go through all the feelings of responsibility.

'I sometimes had the nightmare that it had just been a dream, and I had to wake up and find that it really had happened.'

He paused again and absently picked a bag full of toffees from the side-pocket. He offered her one. She shook her head very slowly. He pulled at the cellophane ends, and rolled the toffee into his mouth, pulling it in with his tongue.

'There was one thing that made me think for a while I really was crazy: you remember the boy? The boy in the cage? The mouth open, wide and screaming? Sometimes I dreamt he had been up by the gates of the Old Baths. Sometimes I thought it was part of that morning. I couldn't work him out. Was that me making out it wasn't my fault? Had I invented him? Was I really devil-possessed as those papers said? Was he egging me on?'

Rachel shook her head. 'He would want to

stop you. I know that. Think how he suffered, if that account of the gibbeting's true.'

'I'm pleased you say that. Do you know, I think I've worked a bit more of that out. Just wandering round here, through these few days...'

Rachel looked across and saw the glitter of tears still mixed up with the fair lashes fanning from his lower eyelids.

'Later, much much later, when I was less frightened of them, I started to talk to them, those professionals. I tried to tell them about that feeling. And the boy. Then they really tried to get me to say ... no, that's not fair; I think they'd've been *happier* if I'd said the boy, or his voice made me do it. Egged me on. You know—voices in the head? But it wasn't like that. I knew that then; I know that now.'

'Like I say, maybe the boy was trying to stop you,' said Rachel. 'Maybe he was just sorry for you.'

'Could be that. Maybe sorry for himself,' Alex said absently. 'But he wasn't telling me to do it. Even I didn't tell me to do it. It was done before I even thought. As Jonno was tumbling down from his island in a rain of stones. Maybe that makes me really evil. I worry about that. Even now when I get in a temper, I worry about that, that thing of the second. With Maggie, or with little Charlie. I'll never know. Never be free of that fear.'

Rachel shivered, but pushed on. 'Do you

259

remember what happened afterwards?'

'I remembered hanging onto the clothes which were all gunged up by now. I just hared it. Right up through the back streets. Nobody. Not a soul to see. Right home.' There was pain in his voice, which had gone so low that it was barely audible.

Rachel took a deep breath. 'What then? What happened then?'

'I put the clothes back in the cupboard, got washed again, then took my Nana some tea after her afternoon nap. She commented on how clean I was, but did I know I had a tidemark halfway up my neck?' He unrolled another toffee, and the cheek nearest Rachel bulged out as he started to chew it.

'You know? For the rest of the day I forgot all about the clothes. Put it to the back of my mind and left it. It just lay there like something you've eaten which you know you'll sick up. But you hope that by pretending it's not there it'll go down all the way and won't bother you.

'Then about teatime Nana started to talk about it; got news of it on her own particular bush-telegraph. She had quite a good time, being disgusted about it. I remember her saying they should hang draw and quarter the creature that had done it. So then I had another thought to put away to the back of my head, or the pit of my stomach; wherever the bad memories are stored. That's what they'd do to me. Something like they did to the boy, the boy in the cage.'

'You came to school as though nothing had happened!'

'I had to do that, didn't I? I had "forgotten" what happened. Nothing had really happened, except in that pit at the very back of my mind.'

'But it did come back to you, because of the clothes.' Rachel paused. 'Because of me.'

'That's one way to look at it. The taking and burning the clothes: I did that in a kind of haze. Then their significance came back to the front of my mind and I came to your house. I'd've sicked it up sooner or later. One thing: it strikes me now, looking at the me I was then, I don't think I really knew I had ... killed them. I didn't really know what "dead" was...'

Rachel sat quietly for a few seconds. 'Poor little things,' she said, 'just playing, then...'

'Yeah,' he said grimly, his mouth pulled hard back against his teeth.

They looked out of the car into a world swimming in a wash of rain, the painful silence between them enduring several minutes.

Rachel finally, with a great effort, broke it. 'Was it terrible? In the places they put you?'

'Terrible? Well they handled me like I was a firebolt for a while. It was ages before I would talk—tell anybody anything real. Made up stories at first. A lot of folks were curious, like I said, as though I were an object. A strange animal of some kind. Got beaten up quite regularly in a few places. Was adopted in a

261

peculiar fashion by some older lad now and then. But I got my food. Cleanish clothes and bed. There was a kind of school. There were the workshops. Not that much worse than before. In some ways better. At one point I decided it was useful to be strong, so I started to work out—when I was about thirteen or fourteen, I think. Been doing it ever since. Useful to be strong because it means you're almost never challenged. Still, right through, I was on my own a lot. People came and went and I was always there, in one place or another. I was alone too, because of the ... peculiarity ... of what I'd done.'

'What about you yourself? What did *you* think about what you'd done?'

He turned in the car to face her. His eyes, the now-remembered silver blue, looked at her unblinking. 'I just locked it away and tried to survive. It's only now I really know. And I'm terrified. Terrified of myself and what I've done to Jonno and Mikey. There's no way I can go back. No way I can make up.'

He started on another toffee. 'I think about that cage, and the boy. Like I said, I wonder now if that violence is still in me. I saw my grandmother the other day and I was angry with her; for who she was, for leaving me to rot. A split second, I could have hit her.'

'We all feel like that about someone, from time to time,' interposed Rachel.

He shrugged. 'As it was I gave her a
262

mouthful. A filthy prison mouthful. But really, I never know. Sometimes like I said, I look at Maggie and Charlie and Sophie and I'm terrified. Of myself. They say that it won't happen, and I have to believe them. But...'

'But you studied in prison? Made something of yourself there.'

'After a good while, it wasn't so bad. I was used to things. I could do courses and prove I wasn't a dummy. I could hold my own with the others. Then this bloke started to come and talk to me. Alex Van Dorn. The man whose name I have taken. He'd been some kind of shrink after being a prisoner of war. Retired by then. He visited me for years while I was in, and helped me set up when I came out. I still see him, but he's really old and frail now. Maggie was another of his protegées. Not like me though. Just out of her skull on drugs. Mr Van Dorn sometimes says she and I are an example of when the blind lead the blind to some success.'

Alex reached over to the back seat and brought out a large folding umbrella, making Rachel jump. He smiled slightly at her, appreciating her nervousness. 'Now I've told you more or less everything, I want to show you something. Do you think you could survive this downpour?'

She nodded, then waited till he came round to her side of the car, holding the umbrella aloft to afford some protection.

He led her through the tall gates into the graveyard, which was covered with deep meadow grass, untrimmed and left to grow wild. Here and there, the gravestones jutted out of the straggling grass. Some headstones were quite recent, bright and hard letters giving dates from the last fifty years. Some of them were so old that the lettering merely rendered a bumpy surface on the old stone.

The rain sustained its steady effort to flatten the world. Ignoring the seepage into her stout shoes, Rachel pushed her way through the long grass. Ian scrambled along beside her, trying to keep the big umbrella over both their heads.

At one point he stopped walking and touched touching her elbow to pull her back. A yard away, crouching in some flattened grass, was a black bird, a crow, sitting solidly, the rain plopping on and off its feathers. They waited for it to flutter away at their presence, but it stayed its ground, staring back at them with uncaring eyes.

'His territory, I think,' said Alex, walking around the bird with some care. 'His mate'll be somewhere here. You never see one without the other. Like swans.'

This wasn't Ian Sobell speaking, Rachel thought. This was Alex Van Dorn; who had grown, had deliberately changed himself into a new person. This new person who knew about birds, and about other important and unimportant things, in a measure and proportion which were unique to Alex Van Dorn. He had been creating himself while she, half-destroyed by the event of that Sunday, had limped along with half a life.

He finally came to a halt beside a large tabletop grave deep in the shadow of the church wall. 'Here. I've been digging around while I've been in the town. Old books and maps and the other things, in the public library. Trying to put things in their place. Did you know, in that place where the Baths were, there was a field called Three Spike? And here is something else from the old time.'

Rachel leaned across the mossy surface. It was very old, but the lettering had been recently cleared out, and was not difficult to read:

HERE LIE THE BODIES OF
JANE AND MADOC TRENT
CHILDREN OF REUBEN TRENT
Killed in their innocence
By their father's servant
Philip Wales, who was executed
For this deed

'See this as well? "Erected by subscription..." much later? A hundred years after, I should think. Me, I think this is the boy, Miss Waterman. The boy in the gibbet. The boy I read about in class that day; the boy I saw that once. He told me the names Jane and Madoc. I told you I'd seen him, that day before the police came. He told me the story; how it happened. This thing here with Jane and Madoc.'

She looked at the shadowy letters and then back into his anxious face.

'What did he want with me? Was it because he was a m-murderer too? Should this make me even more certain of the evil of what I did that day being a kind of returning circle?' The voice, stripped of the veil of its West Country accent, sounded hard and desperate. 'That I'll be wandering round in three hundred years trying to tell my side of the story?'

The wind started to swirl around them, blowing the excess rain from the grass across their bodies and into their faces, in spite of the protecting umbrella. They ran to the car together. Ian stood with the umbrella while she got into the passenger seat, then went round and jumped in on his side, shaking the umbrella outside the car with vigorous efficiency. When this business was achieved they sat together in a silence eventually broken by Rachel.

'I don't know what you want me to say Ian. If you like I will say I think he was around then, and I think he has been around now.'

'Around?'

'The last few days he's been around here. I've sensed him too. Like you. Maybe like you he wants somebody to know, to understand.

Or maybe he saw what you did and has taken on your guilt too. Maybe he wants me to understand about you. Now you've told me your story, like he told you his.'

'Maybe he wanted to say even after all this time, that he wasn't evil; just another poor bloody human being ... That's like me, sure enough.' He broke off and turned to reach a brown paper parcel tied with red string from the back seat. 'Here. This is the present I brought for you.'

Taking off her gloves off, she undid the string with great care and pulled away the brown paper from a shoe box. Moving some tissue to one side, she brought out a squat figure carved in wood.

'I started it one time in prison, when I wrote you a letter. Then it went to one side for years and years, because I couldn't just get onto it. Then four, five months ago I came across the wood, and was pulled into finishing it. I've worked on it in my spare time ever since.'

She passed one hand right over and down the figure. It was beautifully made and finished, the grain subtly enhanced by careful polishing. There was the short square frame, the thick unkempt hair. The feet were bare. The shoulders were covered by a short jerkin. The face was round, the cheeks high and flat. It was the face she had seen several times in the last week. The face of Philip Wales, called Pip.

'It's the boy,' she said. 'It's Philip Wales.

267

Pip.'

'Yes,' he said, 'You know his name. Pip ...
You really have seen him! I don't have to
explain. You're not going to tell me I'm crazy.'
His voice was relieved, jubilant.

'But why ... how did this come about? This
figure?'

'He just grew up under my hands. I'd even
forgotten that it was you I'd started that piece
for. I just worked on and started to wonder
where I'd seen the face before. Just a general
sort of interest. I didn't know what I'd do with
the figure. Sell it probably. Never thought
about you. Mostly I try to keep all that stuff
behind me. Not forget; you can't do that
entirely. But try to go forward. Damage
limitation. Anyway, when he was finally
finished, I saw who he was. I knew, then, he
was for you, and I knew I'd have to bring him.'

She stroked her finger down the face, the
broad figure. 'He had such a terrible time. Just
a boy ... innocent in all but that terrible act.
Suffered enough for both of you, I should
think. Maybe that's what he's bringing to you
now: some kind of freedom from the cage.
Maybe for me too.'

'But that about him? Still somewhere,
somehow screaming...'

'No. Not now. I'm sure not now. You've
been able to tell your story, to me just now,
and, in whatever versions to all those other
people those years ago. You listened to him. I

listened to you. He wanted that. Maybe the circle is complete.' She shivered briefly. 'And here, in your carving, he has his memorial, showing him as a vulnerable human being, not some satanic creature. He's not tied down now; he can go. He's not screaming any more.'

His hand came over hers, where she grasped the figure. It was thin but very strong and very warm. 'Miss Waterman, you're all right. You are all right! I knew then, ignorant, innocent misbegotten kid that I was; I know now. Now I've got to go, or I'll get shot. That Maggie has some kind of temper, I can tell you. Where do you want to go? Back home?'

'Well, home first. I want to telephone someone called Daisy Montague to see if she would like a ride in my new car on Sunday. Did I say I was going to get a new car? Then I'll get on to school. I can't wait to get on with things. There's so much to do. A life to live.'

She put the small figure carefully back into its box, placing it neatly under its tissue paper. Then she rewrapped the box in its brown paper and red string. Each act was radiant with finality.

Alex Van Dorn, nee Ian Sobell, put the car into gear, reversed with a rather dramatic scream of tyres and roared away. As he did so, first one, then a second crow alighted on the ornate gatepost. Soon the rain stopped and the graveyard returned to its still, dark normality.

269